And a House with a White Picket Fence

One Woman's destructive search for a love life with greener pastures

Leah M. McClure

DEDICATION

To my Husband, my children and everyone who reminded me that I could
and more importantly, that I should.

CONTENTS

ACKNOWLEDGMENTS

My editor Robin Baum .

1 MY NORMAL

My muffled moans can be heard throughout the corridors as I lie panting uncontrollably. "I need to push," I cry out. "Not yet, Mrs. Wayland," answers the nurse. The other two nurses are busy dropping the bottom of my birthing bed out, preparing me for the magic moment. My doctor enters the room, "Do I have time to change?" "Not if you want to see a baby being born!" answers one of the nurses as she pushes a hide-away desk full of instruments up to him.

I look over my right shoulder at my husband Joseph. He has an amazingly calm look on his face as he squeezes my hand. In the midst of all the confusion and pain, I'm glad to see he hasn't lost it. I feel as though any minute now, I just might. "Oh, God, I need to push!" I warn. "Hold on, Mrs. Wayland, hold on," says the nurse as she spreads my thighs apart to look for the baby's head. "Dr. Harvey, she's crowning." Dr. Harvey then drops himself into the swivel chair in front of me and takes over. "Now, I want you to wait for your next contraction and give me a big push, Taylor. Just listen to your body." As my body kicks in like clockwork, I begin to push. I'm now thinking, I must have been crazy to go through this a third time. I wonder how my two daughters, Bailey and Dawn, will like their new sibling.

"The head's out," says Dr. Harvey. There is a mad rush to clear the baby's nose and mouth. I notice Joseph peeking over to see his child as I take a deep breath, preparing to deliver our child fully into this world. I grit my teeth and push with all my might as I feel my child slipping out. I have been blessed with a new life. A son. His name is Joe Jr.. I lay there embracing my husband, tearful with joy, and think to myself, this is normal. It's all I've ever wanted out of life - a sense of normalcy.

I can remember as far back as pre-kindergarten thinking, 'when I grow up, I want to be a wife and a mother.' Although I heard this clearly in my head, I never expressed it to the teacher or my class. Even at the ripe old age of four I knew those goals weren't appropriate for a child my age. Being a scrawny kid with glasses made me different enough already!

I grew up in a small town in Connecticut, the third of four children. My parents were David and Vera Salters. While my parents had loved one another at one time, they didn't by the time I came along. When it came to raising us, I honestly believe they did the best they could. But as an adult and with a family of my own, I can't help but feel that their best wasn't good enough.

My mother is a recovering alcoholic and drug addict. During her periods of dependency, my father was as co-dependent as they come. Ironically, my father wonders how in the world my sister, Deandra, could stand a man who is an alcoholic! My older brother, Adam, is my parent's pride and joy, and a prime example of success. Adam has compensated for my parent's lack of attention with his academic achievements and, boy, has he thrived! My younger brother is still at home with my parents. I really feel for him, because he's stuck there in the midst of the madness. Although my parents' situation is not extreme, it has had a very profound impact on Deandra, Adam, Lawrence and me.

2 HAVING IT ALL

It's Sunday morning, and I'm sitting in the front room with my children. Bailey, six, and Dawn, four, are hard at play as I nurse Joe Jr..

As I'm gazing through the front window, I notice Janice ("Janny") Colebury drive up. Janice and I have been close friends for six years. We met soon after I moved to Virginia. She was pregnant with her six-year-old daughter, Jolie, at the same time that I was with Bailey. Our children were born within two hours of each other. People often make fun of us because our lifestyles are so different. They call us the 'old married couple.' Janny is a career woman first, a mommy second, and a wife, third. And everyone knows it! She is tall, fair-skinned and very attractive.

She always keeps her hair very short, to the dismay of her husband, Coleman.

In the front seat with Janny is Daneka Smith. Daneka works as a writer for La Negra magazine. She's the political one in our circle of friends. Daneka is dark-skinned, stocky, and stands five feet even. She always wears African-inspired garments. Daneka is single, opinionated and outspoken; her personality often dominates the conversation. She's deeply committed to the advancement of African-Americans in all areas of life. Many of her efforts are in support of children's interests, which I admire. I wish I had her drive.

And, of course, in the back seat is Beatrice Arthur, 'Tricie' as we call her. Tricie generally demands most of our collective time and energy. Her life is always a mess. She married very young, at 18. She had two children by the time she was 21, and was divorced by 22. Her husband left her for her sister. Since her divorce, she's had one failed relationship after another. Tricie is brown-skinned and usually wears her hair back in a ponytail. She has blue eyes like her mother. She is bi-racial and proud of it, which makes for some good confrontations between Tricie and

Daneka. Tricie has decided that all black men are like her ex-husband, so she will only date white men in the future.

Janny and Daneka step out of the car and walk toward the house as Tricie follows behind. "How are you feeling?" Janny asks as she opens the door to the front room. "Let me see that little man," Daneka says as she sits alongside me. Tricie comes in and immediately speaks to Bailey and Dawn. "I feel awful," admits Janny. "I had to call Joseph this morning to find out whether you had a boy or a girl. Your delivery took place in the middle of my meeting with the district supervisor."

"Yes, Janny, that is awful," Daneka retorts. "I don't even know how you could admit to it." Tricie adds, "You and that damn job, Janice." I look over at Beatrice, anticipating the remark that's going to come from Janice. "That damn job is the reason why I drive a Mercedes, live in a $500,000 home and send my daughter to the best private school in the state!" I can't resist joining in. "What about Coleman?" I ask with a smirk on my face, "What did you pay for him?" Janny and Tricie smile back at me. "Don't start, Taylor," Janny threatens.

"So what are you going to do tonight, Taylor?" Daneka asks. "I think I'll just chill out a bit. Joseph is supposed to be taking Bailey and Dawn to Chuck E. Cheese, so Joe Jr. and I will just relax and bond a little." Tricie sighs. "You're so lucky, Taylor," she says, "I never got any help from David. You've got a nice home, three beautiful children…" Daneka interrupts, "Yeah, and they look surprisingly like the mailman!" Janny sits down and laughs. "No, really," continues Tricie, "Joe is good to you." She stands up, walks over to me and takes the baby from my arms, "You're totally doing that white-picket-fence thing!" As I listen, I stare through the window into the yard and think about how 'average' has always been a welcome idea to me. When I was growing up, I yearned to do those normal things that other kids did with their parents. Nothing extraordinary; just everyday, normal family activities. Now, as an adult, it appears that I'm doing those things. My dearest friends believe it. Hell, even my husband and children believe it. But there is still an empty place inside me, and I have no clue what's supposed to fill it…

"Taylor? … Taylor?" Janice taps me on the shoulder, "I said I've got to go. I have a board meeting at one o'clock." "I'm sorry,

I'm just a little tired," I apologize. "Hey, I'll call you later," says

Daneka. "Please don't," I beg, "I'm taking the phone off the hook

so I can get some rest!" Tricie kisses me on the cheek. "OK, we'll

see you tomorrow." As they walk down the porch steps to the car,

Bailey pulls on my shirt asking, "Mommy, can we take a nap?" I

wave good-bye to my friends and say to my daughter, "You bet,

pumpkin." As the car pulls away, I think to myself, 'I'm so tired.

I'm just so tired.'

Later that evening, I awaken as Joseph walks into the room

taking his shirt off. Joe is six-foot-six and 230 pounds, with plenty

of muscles that add to his stature. His beautiful dark-skinned bare

chest glistens under the light. His leg muscles cut through the

Calvin Klein® bike-short style underwear he is wearing. Smooth

skin, a clean-shaven face… yum, a tasty sight! "Where are the

girls?" I ask. "They're asleep," answers Joe. "Where's Joe Jr.?"

"He's asleep, too," he says as he crawls on the bed and lies on top

of me. "Where's Taylor?" he asks mockingly. "I don't know, but I

hear she may still be at the hospital with your son!" I answer,

running my nails up his back. "What do you say we torture

ourselves?" Joseph asks as he unbuttons my blouse. I smile at him and use my feet to pull down his sweatpants. He's so handsome,

and that hard body! Not too big, not too small; making love to him

is never a chore. He begins to kiss my collarbone as he pushes his

hand under my bra, unhooking it with a twist of his thumb. Our

labored breathing is getting heavier. Using his knee to spread my

legs apart, I can feel his erection rubbing up against me. I press my

head back against the pillow, all the while thinking, 'this is

torture.' At that moment, Joseph lowers himself with gentle kisses

around my nipples. My moans of pleasure are in sync with each

pet. I thrust my hand down into his pants to massage his bare ass.

To reciprocate, Joe thrusts his tongue deeper into my mouth while

pulling my leg up beside him, our bodies now mimicking

lovemaking. I then reached around to caress his dick, up and down,

with every stroke bringing him closer to ejaculating. After pulling

my hand away, he once again runs his tongue down my neck,

across my breasts, down my abdomen, even teasing me with kisses

on my inner thigh, not leaving an inch avoided. The feel of his

hand, up and down my back and across my ass, is gentle enough to

send me into climactic heaven. By now I have a fistful of the

sheets and my other hand is gripping his muscular arm. His sweat rolls down his rippling muscles and drips from his body onto mine. I push him over, lie on top of him and begin to lick his chest. Joe pulls me up to his face, kissing me with raw passion. He is so hard I don't think he'll last another second. While gliding my tongue across his chest, I once again reach down into his pants. Not wanting to come all over himself, Joe pushes my hand away, but I insist, this time kissing lower and lower across his stomach, making a beeline for that wonderful shaft. Under Joe's moans, we hear a muffled voice call, "Daddy . . . Daddy." I look up and there is Dawn, standing in the doorway half asleep.

Joe scrambles under the sheet for his sweat pants. We look at each other and smile. "Hold that thought," he says as he jumps out of bed to grab Dawn and tuck her back into her bed. When he returns to the bed, Joe begins to kiss me with a smirk on his face. He then stops, rubs the side of my face, looks deep into my eyes and says, "God, you're beautiful... I'm so lucky." If it weren't for my still-healing body, we would have made love all night. Instead, we do exactly what Joseph proposed. We torture each other for hours, kissing, rubbing, sucking and grinding. Joe's touch still makes me shudder with passion. He's so good to me. Tricie is right.

3 GROWN-UP TIME

"Mommy, are you going to have another baby?" Bailey asks me.
She loves her sister and brother dearly. If it were up to Bailey and
her father, I'd be having babies annually. "Not anytime soon,
sweetie." That answer will hold her for at least 30 seconds.

We always have in-depth conversations on our way to
school. Bailey and Dawn attend Martinique School, the best
private, and predominantly black, school in Virginia. Bailey is in
the first grade and Dawn is in Junior Kindergarten. The two of
them generally enjoy school. As we pull up to the front of the
Lower School, the assistant teacher, Ms. Brown, walks up to the
car door. "I don't want to go, Mommy," pouts Dawn. "Not again,
Dawn," says Bailey, shrugging her shoulders as she exits the car.
"Good morning, Mrs. Wayland, will you be leaving Joe Jr. today?"

Ms. Brown asks. "Yes, and I think my baby girl may need a little help today," I gesture with my eyes toward Dawn. Ms. Brown gathers up Joe Jr. and takes Dawn by the hand. "I think I may need your help with your baby brother today, Dawn. Will you help me?" she coaxes. Dawn nods in agreement. I watch the three of them walk into the building.

Now that the children are at school, I have five and a half hours to play grown up. I'm on my way downtown for a cup of tea. It's something I enjoy – just sitting and doing something that requires little or no thought. While driving downtown, I'm trying to decide which teahouse I want to visit this time. Chachos and Teariffic are my favorites.

It's a clear and sunny day, and all the beautifully kept shrubs and rose bushes along the sides of the street are blooming. Teariffic has an outdoor patio, so that's where I've decided to go. I pull up about a block away and park. I walk up to the building and am met at the door by Kimberly, the hostess, who also happens to be my babysitter.

"Good morning, Mrs. Wayland, will you be having breakfast?" she asks. "No, Kim, just tea, thanks," I answer.

"Inside or out?" Kim wants to know. "I think I'll sit outside today," I respond. She leads me outside. "How are the kids?" she asks. "Great," I answer while taking off my jacket, "in fact, I may be planning a dinner party this weekend. Can you babysit?" She smiles. "Just give me a call." I sit down at the table she indicates. "I'll have a regular tea with plenty of sugar and milk, please."

As I begin to people-watch my mind wanders back to when I was a child going to school. I don't really have any magical memories of my school days. A lot of it was a nightmare, really. I was skinny before it became a fashion statement, wore glasses, and was painfully shy. My Dad worked two jobs and my mother worked full time, when she was up to it. This usually meant I got myself ready for school. It also meant that a lot of things slipped their minds – like the fact that there was no milk, bread, or cereal in the house for weeks at a time. And soap, lotion and hair grease were an occasional luxury. I'd like to think that my parents worked that hard to make sure the bills got paid, and that the other needs simply fell below the radar. Whatever the reason, it's why I decided to put my career on hold while my children are young; so that I can be fully available for my husband and family.

"Taylor . . . Taylor." I look up and Coleman is standing before me. "Hi, Coleman, what are you doing over here at this time of the morning?" I ask. "I was supposed to meet Janice for breakfast, but she got pulled away to Norfolk for the day," he answers. "Sit down," I invite. "Thanks. What are you having?" he asks. "Just tea. Will you have some with me?" "Yeah, I think I will," he says. He waves at the waitress, who comes over. "I'll have rose tea with lemon, please," Coleman orders.

"So, how is Joe Jr. doing? It seems like he was just born a week ago," he commented. "I know. He's getting so big," I answer. "I remember when Jolie was born," Coleman says. "I just wanted her to stay a little baby for the first five years, and then I would decide whether or not she was allowed to grow up!" He smiles, and I smile back.

Coleman is an old friend of Joe's, and an easy person to like. He is also drop-dead gorgeous. He stands six-foot-three and is very fair-skinned, with light brown eyes and dusty brown curly hair that he keeps very short. Today he is wearing very worn oversized jeans, a white shirt and a color-blocked tie. His denim baseball cap is as faded as his jeans. Janny hates when he dresses in his "hip-hop" attire. She always wants him to wear slacks. I think he looks great. Janice is lucky to have a man who is dedicated to his family, but her mind is so clouded with her job that she doesn't have time to appreciate him.

"Janice told me something about dinner at your house this weekend," Coleman says as the waitress brings over his tea. "I just wanted to have everyone over. I thought it might be fun to put Daneka and Tricie in the mud pit for entertainment." We laugh.

"How's Joe doing?" Coleman asks. "I want to get him over to the house to help me work on my deck." "He's doing great," I answer, "He's going down to Atlanta in a few weeks for some workshop – on storing chemicals, or destroying chemicals, or something. That just shows you how much I know about my husband's profession." "Don't feel bad," comforts Coleman. "I haven't the slightest idea what my wife does all day long. I just know that it keeps her away from Jolie and me." He gives me a half-hearted smile, but I can see some sadness behind his eyes.

I know how Coleman feels. I fantasize about the perfect marriage, with the perfect spouse, great kids, and lots of material things. We both have most of that. And yet, while I've spent a good part of my 26 years of life trying to figure out what I want, Coleman already knows what he wants. It would be ideal if he could get his wife to want those same things, in the same order of priority.

"Wait a minute; which week is Joe going to be in Atlanta?" Coleman asks. "The week of the 23rd," I answer. "Janice is going to be in Chicago that week," he says, and then sips his tea. "Would you like me to take Jolie to school?" I offer. "That'd be great. I'm supposed to work on the Madison building," he says. "You got that contract?" I ask. "Yeah, we won the bid last Friday." "That's great, Coleman, I'm so happy for you! Janny was just talking to me about that bid a few days ago. She must be so glad . . . for you, I mean," I say as I stand up, lean over and pat him on the shoulder. "Thanks, Taylor."

We smile for a moment and I think about the conversation Janny and I had about the Madison contract. She feels that he needs to move on to bigger and better things, rather than accepting small projects here and there that look like 'odd jobs.'

"Listen, I'd better run," Coleman says as he stands. "I need to get home and work on some of my paperwork." I stand. "Thanks

17

for joining me, Coleman." We hug goodbye. "I'll see you and Janny Saturday night." "What time?" Coleman asks. "Around seven o'clock," I answer. "See you then, Taylor." Coleman walks away. I finish my cup of tea, thinking over what the menu will be for Saturday night. I love entertaining. I love my friends dearly and it pleases me to have us all together.

4 DINNER WITH OLD FRIENDS

I stand in front of the mirror pulling up my thigh-high hose as Joseph comes up from behind and hugs me, running his hands up my legs. "You know what these do to me?" I turn around to kiss him. He presses his lips firmly against mine and I close my eyes to deepen the kiss. In a flash, I see Coleman's face. I jerk away from Joseph in shock and open my eyes. "What's wrong?" Joe asks. Looking deep into his puzzled eyes, and wondering where in the hell that came from, I come up with, "I was just wondering if the caterer will remember those little chocolate mint things everyone always asks about." "Are you serious?" Joe questions. "Well, they forgot them last time and I just don't want – well, I just hope they remember to bring them," I say, pulling away. Joe wipes his mouth with a smirk and pats me on my behind as he walks away.

'I must have been thinking about Coleman because we had tea the other day,' I think to myself. I reach for my sleeveless black dress and step into it. It's a very close-fitting, mid-thigh short dress cut very low in the front to show cleavage (if I had any). This is one of my favorite black dresses. The part of me that is a tease adores this dress.

The doorbell rings. "Joe, get that please. It's Kim." Kim is a gem of a baby sitter. She always made it easy for us to not worry about the kids. "Kimmy, Kimmy!" Bailey and Dawn yell, running past my door and down the hall. "Hi, girls, where's your brother?" Kim asks as she peeks into my room. "Hi, Mrs. Wayland, you look great!" "Thanks, Kim," I say, turning around while putting an earring into my ear. "Can you stay the night?" "Sure. Do you mind if I braid their hair?" she asks. "No, please do," I respond. "Oh, by the way," Kim remembers as she grabs the hair grease and the comb off my dresser, "I got accepted to Spellman." "Congratulations, Kim! Any thoughts on what your major might be?" Kim smiles. "I'll take the girls downstairs. They're so sweet."

Just then the doorbell rings and Kim opens the door to Daneka. "Hi, Kim," Daneka says. "Hi, Daneka, you look great, too! Boy, you old broads give me something to look forward to!"

Kim smiles and continues with the children to the basement.

"Where's Taylor?" Daneka asks. "I'm coming down now," I yell.

Daneka is wearing an African-inspired printed pant set with a headdress. The colors are a mixture of browns, blacks, and greens. Her braids are wrapped into the headdress. She is wearing a button on her shirt that reads "Always 4 Real." And that's Daneka, wrapped up in three words. As I come down the stairs, Joe comes from the kitchen and greets Daneka with a hug. "What's up, girl?" he asks. "Nothing much, Joe. You look good! Been working out?" Daneka asks. "Well, you know I gotta keep my women happy," he responds. "Please!" I say, pushing him aside as I hug Daneka. "What's going on, girl?" I ask. "Nothing really. I've been trying to get them to let me take the trip to South Africa, but I think they're going to let Shirley go." Shirley has been working at La Negra five years longer than Daneka and often gets the plum assignments.

"What are you drinking, ladies?" Joe asks. "Wine," Daneka answers. His eyes move to me. "Me, too," I say. As he turns his back, the doorbell rings. It's Tricie and (of course) her date of the week. "Hi!" Tricie says cheerfully, rushing into the house. "Taylor, I want you to meet Andrew."

Blonde hair and blue eyes. 'Please, Lord, if Daneka makes it through the evening, I owe you one,' I think. "... and Andrew," Tricie continues, "this is Taylor, and ... uh, Daneka." I extend my hand to shake his. "It's nice to meet you, Andrew," Daneka says, shaking his hand as Tricie looks on cautiously and takes off her jacket. "How are you doing?" Daneka asks. "Fine, thank you," Andrew answers.

Joseph then re-enters with our drinks and says hello to Tricie and Andrew. He then disappears with Andrew as Tricie, Daneka and I find our way into the living room like three schoolgirls. "So," I ask, "where did you meet Andrew?" Tricie folds her arms, takes a deep breath, sits back in the chair and looks at Daneka, then back at me. "Ya know, he really is a very sweet guy," she says, trying to convince herself as much as us. "I just wanted to know where you met him, Tricie. It couldn't have been too long ago; I just talked to you on Thursday," I say. "I knew him then, I just ... didn't want to go through, you know ... this!" Tricie says throwing her hands in my direction. "We want the best for you, Trese," Daneka comments. "Really?" Tricie questions, "And I suppose I can only find that in a brotha, right?"

"Listen to me, Beatrice," Daneka confronts, "you came here ready to face off, which tells me that you aren't even secure with your own decisions. Now, my opinion about your dates shouldn't affect your choices, but it should make you realize that it's not just the color of their skin that bothers me. It's the fact that a mistake one black man made with you a long time ago has turned you against all black men on principle! Now, have a drink and tell us where you met Andrew." Tricie sits back, and with a distressed look on her face, says "I, uh … I'm … what're you drinking?"

Tricie means so much to us, but she has so much to learn about relationships. We all feel compelled to teach her and maybe help her avoid any more pitfalls. But in truth, what we really need to do is back off and let her learn, and to give opinions and advice only when we are called upon.

The doorbell rings again. I answer the door. It's Janny, Coleman and Jolie. Janny looks casual for a change. Of course, 'casual' for Janny is still quite dressy for most of us. She's wearing a long black dress with a turtleneck. "Hey, guys!" I say to Janny and Coleman while giving her a hug. I bend over close to Jolie's face. "Miss Jolie, would you like to go play with Bailey, Dawn and Joe Jr.?" "Yes, Mrs. Wayland. Do you like my party dress?" she asks. "Oh, of course, Jolie, you can never have too many Nubian princess dresses!"

Janny and Coleman walk into the living room. "How are you doing, Coleman?" I ask. "Hanging in there, Taylor. Is Joe back here?" he asks walking toward the den. "Yes, he disappeared with your coat." Coleman was wearing his bucks, blue Dockers® and a white shirt. I know Janny asked him to wear this outfit. He looks great, but it's so obvious whenever Janny picks his clothes out.

I follow Janny into the living room. She has instinctively placed herself between Tricie and Daneka. "You want a glass of wine?" I ask Janny. "Yes, that'd be great," she answers. I go to the kitchen to get a bottle of wine from on top of the refrigerator. I pull a chair up close to the refrigerator door and stand on top of it. After grabbing the bottle, I step down from the chair, but my dress catches on the handle of the refrigerator door, exposing most of my backside! I'm tugging at my dress trying to unhook it from the door when I realize someone is behind me. I look around and notice Coleman standing in the doorway with his arms folded, an empty glass dangling from one hand and a smile on his face. I realize that he still has a full view of my ass since my dress is still caught on the handle. I'm deeply embarrassed, but the only thing I can do is smile, and he readily smiles back. Finally, I get my dress loose, almost tearing it. "You know; I don't normally invite my old friends over to show them my underwear." Coleman walks up to me and whispers in my ear, "Don't worry; thigh-highs don't do much for me!" I slap him on the arm as he covers his mouth with laughter. "Take this to your wife," I say handing him the bottle of wine.

My skin is hot, and I'm mortified. If I were white, my skin would be bright red. I feel like a schoolgirl with a crush. What the hell am I talking about? I *do* have a crush on Coleman, always have. Or maybe I've been sipping a little too much wine…

The party lasts until the wee hours of the morning. For dinner we have seafood crepes, lobster patties, plenty of shrimp (Joe's favorite), fresh salad, and Janny's sweet potato pie for dessert. And of course, there are plenty of drinks for everyone.

This is how I spend the majority of my weekends: enjoying the company of my family and friends. My mother often tells me she thinks I'm not spending enough time on myself – that I'm doing more for everyone else than for me. But in my mind, I'm doing exactly what I want to do – what makes me happy.

I'm a housewife, and taking care of others is my job. I think my mother remembers how life was when it was *her* job. She missed a lot of her young adult years. If she could start over, I think she would do things differently. I believe she would definitely change the timing.

5 PICNICS AND ROMANCE

Tomorrow is Sunday, an official day of rest. I decide to make up a picnic basket and spend the day with my family at the park. I've never cared much for the great outdoors, but Joe and the kids enjoy it tremendously, so I'm content to do it for them.

I always feel proud when I step back and observe my little family. I sometimes watch them playing, reading a story, eating dinner, or just moving about the house, and it's almost as if I'm removed from them. At these times I think to myself, 'look what I've done.' Despite this sense of accomplishment, I often feel empty and have a desire to try to create what I feel is missing.

My clock reads 7:30 a.m. I sit straight up in bed, wipe my eyes and reach for my robe. "What time is it?" Joe asks. "Early. I'm just going downstairs to pack a basket before the kids get up." With that, Joe rolls over, cuddles up with his pillow and falls back to sleep.

I quietly walk past the girls' room, look in, and notice that Bailey is now facing the foot of her bed with one leg hanging off. At some point Dawn had climbed out of her bed and into Bailey's. She is lying beside her sister with her thumb in her mouth. I pull the door shut and continue down the hall to Joe Jr.'s room. He is beginning to squirm. It's almost time for his eight o'clock feeding.

I rush down the stairs, picking up little bits of Bailey and Dawn's clothing as I go. Sitting at the bottom of the stairs on the right, I see Kim putting her shoes on and gathering up a pile of folded blankets. "Good morning, Mrs. Wayland, I was just going to wake you," she says. "Good morning, Kim, thanks so much for last night," I say, getting some money out of my wallet and handing it to her. "No problem, I had a great time, and the food was great!" She looks at the amount of money I gave her. "Mrs. Wayland, this is too much. Mrs. Colebury paid me already for Jolie." "I know. Use it for school supplies," I say. She smiles and gives me a hug, and I walk her to the door.

I head for the kitchen, where I begin to gather things for our outing: grapes, crackers, cheese, cookies (chocolate chip of course), strawberries and a few cans of soda. I reach for the picnic basket, which is usually stored below the sink, and remember that it's now on top of the refrigerator because Dawn has decided it makes a wonderful bassinet for her dollies. I place all the snacks inside and add napkins, straws, cups, juice boxes, plastic utensils and paper plates.

As I pack, I'm thinking about the many picnics Joseph and I have taken together. One in particular always comes to mind. It's August 1987. I was 18 years old. Joseph and I had only been dating for a month. That morning I was rushing to get ready for work, and was late as usual. I pulled my jacket on over my shoulders and shoved my feet into my shoes. Racing down my apartment hallway, I grabbed my purse off the couch and my keys off the desk. I pulled the front door open and began the run for the elevator, and immediately collided with Joseph as he was getting ready to knock on the door. The impact knocked a picnic basket and bottle of wine out of his hand. "I'm so sorry, Joseph! What are you doing here? How long have you been here?" I asked. "I just got here," he answered. "I thought I'd surprise you with an afternoon lunch at Deer Park." He and I began to gather the fruit and sandwiches that had fallen out of the basket. I reached for the rolling bottle of wine (unbroken, I'm relieved to see) and realize that it's Peach Riunite. Anyone who knows anything about me knows it's my favorite wine. I looked up and smiled at Joseph from my kneeling position. "Joe, this is my favorite."

"I know," he answers. "I would have called to let you know that I was planning this for you, Taylor, but honestly, until I saw that bottle of wine on the shelf, I hadn't planned anything." He puts the basket down and kneels close to me, framing my face with both his hands. "If I could feel the way I feel when I'm with you for the rest of my life, it would be just about all that I could stand. Taylor, you're the only girl I know whose beauty really does come from inside. I will never feel like this for anyone else. Do you feel the same?"

I kissed him without answering. That didn't mean that I didn't feel the same as Joe; I was just so overwhelmed by his sentiment that my first and only reaction was to kiss him. Back then, most of my reactions and decisions were based on emotion.

This man was the exact opposite of my father, and that's what I was looking for.

Needless to say, I went with Joe for that picnic. I caught hell from my supervisor, but it was well worth it. That was the day I promised to marry Joseph, and I kept my promise. Joe still makes references to August 1987. He remembers it as well as I do. Being in love with him was so simple then, almost like breathing. It was just that natural. Now, there are times when I have to work at it. I feel guilty about that, so I make sure that we go on lunch outings often. I want him to know that I remember August 1987, too. The only difference today is that now I'm brave enough to answer the question he asked back then.

We spend the day in Charlottesville. Joe Jr. delights us by taking a few steps, with the help of his big sisters, of course. Joseph and I are able to spend some time talking, holding hands and kissing, without work or social interruptions.

While I love my friends dearly, they do take up a great deal of my time. That's probably the one troublesome area in our marriage. And, whenever we fuss about it, deep down inside I actually agree with him. The time I spend entertaining my friends, and his, could instead be devoted to romancing my husband.

Joseph really is much better at the romantic side of our marriage. I'm better at the business side. By this I mean making our marriage, and the household, run smoothly. This is another area where I think I'm a lot like my mother. I believe she spent a great deal of time building her idea of what a marriage was supposed to be, and running the business end, rather than creating a living, breathing connection. I don't want to be like her, because I see where it led. My parents don't have a meaningful relationship; it just looks that way.

Joe and I have real feelings for one another. There is nothing superficial about our marriage. We communicate. Joe is not only very expressive; he's the perfect combination of 'macho' and sensitive. He's a smart, confident, handsome black man who gives one hundred percent to his marriage and still thinks I'm the best thing to happen to him since Wonder Bread.®

And yet, with all this wonderfulness going for us, I still feel some emptiness inside. Why?

6 FLIRTING WITH DANGER

It is 4:47 in the morning, and I awaken to Joseph packing a suitcase. "Where are you going?" I ask while trying to let my eyes adjust to the dimly lit room. He comes over and sits beside me. "Brian just called and I have to go to North Carolina for the night," he says. He rubs my head, which puts me immediately back to sleep.

Joe Jr.'s cries wake me next. When I look up at the clock, it reads 6:49 a.m. My day has officially begun. I get up and walk to his room to find him standing up in his crib, crying angrily at his sisters who have made a Barbie village on the floor. Joe Jr. is reaching out to Bailey as I walk in. "Hi, Mommy. We didn't want to wake you so we decided to come into Joe Jr.'s room and play." Bailey then stands and walks to Joe Jr.'s crib and holds his hand.

"You can stop crying now, Mommy is here." I pick him up and sit him on the floor, which, on a good day would have been more than enough to pacify him, but did not today. I should have known that my husband's abrupt departure was a sign that this day would not be typical.

I spent most the day nursing a very irritable 5½ month-old and trying to occupy his two precocious sisters. It went a little like this: nurse the baby, clean up rooms, breakfast, wash faces, comb hair, get dressed, change diapers, wash laundry, clean house, maintain peace among the natives, nurse the baby, load dishwasher, drop off girls at ballet, wash car, stop at Parcel's Printing, get lunch, nurse the baby, no nap, make hair appointment, change diaper, nurse the baby again, pick up dry cleaning, figure out what to have for dinner, cook dinner, feed the girls. Joe Jr. is so fussy all day that when he falls asleep before dinner and his bath, I'm not about to wake him.

I am just sitting the girls down at the dinner table when the doorbell rings. It's Coleman and Jolie. "Hi, Coleman, hi, Jolie, c'mon in," I invite. Jolie goes to the table to sit with the girls and they begin to chat. "I'm sorry to interrupt your dinner, Taylor, but I promised Joseph that I would drop off these blueprints for the deck. Is he here?" "No, actually, he left to go to North Carolina this morning. Brian called and he packed a bag and left a little before five o'clock this morning. I think he'll be back this . . ." The phone rings. "Excuse me, Coleman."

I answer the phone. It's Joseph calling to tell me that he won't be back until the following afternoon. He gives me the phone number of the hotel where he's staying. "Coleman is here, he is dropping off the blueprints for the deck for you to read... uh, huh... I'll tell him... they're fine... no, they're playing with Jolie... he's asleep... okay... uh, huh... I love you, too."

I hang up the phone and turn to Coleman, who has taken a seat at the table. "Joseph wanted me to tell you that he's sorry but he'll be back tomorrow afternoon and he'll go over the blueprints with you then," I say. Coleman, not looking terribly concerned, says, "that's fine, there's no hurry. Janice is working on her notes tonight, so I thought I'd give her some peace and quiet."

"Has Jolie eaten her dinner yet?" I ask. "Yes, I stopped and picked up some McDonald's on the way over here. I probably should have eaten myself," he says. "I know what you mean," I agree. "I haven't eaten either, and now I'm getting hungry. Let's go pick up Janny and get something to eat." "You better call her first. She had her head buried in paperwork when I left," Coleman suggests.

I call Janice and ask her if she'd like to go out for dinner. She declines, but asks if I can keep Jolie for a while so that she can finish her paper. "Well, you were right, Coleman. Janny's not coming out to play, but if you want, I can call Kim and we can still go get something to eat." "Okay," Coleman says with a solemn look on his face. "Or, we can wait and do this another time when Janny is not so busy," I offer. "I've been waiting for that time for the past six years. I'm hungry now," he retorts.

I call Kim, who comes right over. I change my clothes and Coleman and I head out to Rizzario's Italian Restaurant. I have butterflies in my stomach, the kind you get when you're on a first date. We spend this time getting to know each other better as individuals, as Taylor and Coleman rather than Joe's wife and Janny's husband.

We talk mostly about silly things – the zits we had in high school and the funniest places we fell down in public. But there are revealing moments, too. I realize how lonely Coleman is, although he doesn't say a whole lot about what's lacking in his married life. He insinuates it by saying things like; if Janny had a less hectic schedule he'd take her to Jamaica like she wants. I know that she has already been there on business, but she has never told Coleman because she doesn't want him to feel badly about her having gone without him.

After having dessert and plenty of laughs, we go back to my house so that Coleman can pick up Jolie. As we walk in, there are toys all over the floor and Kim is asleep with the baby monitor by her head. She is startled when I step on Joe Jr.'s rubber squeaky rabbit toy. "Hello, Mrs. Wayland, Mr. Colebury. Where is Mrs. Colebury?" "She's at home working on a paper," Coleman answers. "How were the kids?" I ask. "They were fine. We were watching a Sesame Street tape when we all fell asleep, so I washed them up and put them to bed." I take cash out of my purse and give it to her. Coleman tries to pay her before I do. "I got it," I say, pushing his hand aside. "You paid for dinner," I smile. Kimberly thanks me and leaves.

I take off my coat and as hang it up I notice that Coleman is standing in the same place he was before Kim left. "You might as well let Jolie stay the night. I told Janny that I would keep her for a while." I walk over to Coleman and put my hand on his arm. "Are you okay?" There is a silence. "Sit down, Coleman, I'll be right back."

I go upstairs to check on the girls. They are all in bed fast asleep. I also peek into Joe Jr.'s room. All that crying he did that afternoon has him sleeping like a rock. I look over the banister at Coleman as I go back downstairs. He is sitting with his head in his hands, resting his elbows on his knees. His back is to me.

As I walk around to face him, I can see that he's crying. I sit down next to him on the couch, "What's going on, Coleman?" He looks up, not looking at me right away, and then he turns to me, his face a little red. "Taylor, I know that you and Janny have been friends for a very long time, so you may know her better than I do, and I'm not proud to say that, but, well… has she ever said… does she love me?"

I sigh heavily; relieved that this is a question I can answer. "Coleman, Janny loves you very much. She's just the biggest workaholic I know. She wanted this job, worked hard to get it, and is trying to make sure that she will never lose it. It's the same thing she did with you." I smile and take my hand to turn his face toward mine. "Janny isn't going anywhere. She loves you very much..." I say looking into his eyes.

He still has a very bewildered look on his face, so I hug him. He begins to collapse in my arms as he confesses, "I've never felt that she loves me, Taylor." I hug him tighter to console him. We sit like that for a moment, and it unexpectedly gets very quiet.

Coleman pulls away and looks at me. At first, I just look back into his red, tear-stained eyes, puzzled. Then he slowly leans forward and presses his lips on my cheek, and his tear-stained face moistens mine. He then leans away from my face and raises his left hand to the right side of my neck to pull me closer to him. I can feel the sweat in his palms and his breath on my face. I raise my hand to stop him but inexplicably decide to lay my hand on top of his instead. With my left hand I wipe the tears from his face, leaving my hand there for a moment. His face feels prickly from his five o'clock shadow. With one passionate lunge toward me, he kisses me intensely on the mouth.

My heart is beating so hard I can feel it pulsating against the outside of his jacket. Using what little restraint I have left, I keep my lips shut tight, but I can't resist. Feeling his soft full lips against mine, I wrap my arm around his neck and open my mouth, taking his tongue completely. I can smell his aftershave on my face now. His embrace is strong as he runs his fingers through my hair and holds the back of my neck tightly. He allows himself to explore every inch of my mouth, and I can't free myself from his intoxicating clutch. He places one hand on the small of my back and plants soft kisses starting on one side of my face, across my lips, surging his tongue deep into my mouth, and then kissing again to the other side of my face and down the side of my neck while anchoring me tightly. We kiss passionately, but not lustfully.

Then, both of us, afraid of where this might lead, and at the same moment, try to pull away from each other. The most we can do is pull our lips away. Coleman presses the side of his face against mine, gently caresses my mouth with the tips of his fingers and whispers, "I'm sorry, Taylor, I don't know what came over me."

Feeling ashamed, I don't look at his face. He stands up, goes upstairs to get Jolie and gather up her things, and comes back downstairs to the door. We meet face to face again in dead silence. "We just got caught up in the moment. I feel just as bad as you do," I try to reassure him. "I really am very sorry, Taylor, I... I just am." I just nod my head, acknowledging his response as he walks out.

All that night I thought about what had happened between Coleman and me. Were we really caught up in the moment? Am I trying to conquer him, too? How do I begin to tell my best friend that I intimately kissed her husband? Easy, I decide, I don't.

It's morning and I'm lying still in my bed, not really sleeping, but tired from being awake all night thinking about the connection Coleman and I had shared the night before. I had always flirted with him, not in a sexual way, but more like the way a salesman would flirt with a potential female customer.

I can remember flirting as far back as Janny and Coleman's wedding day. We were all pretty young, early twenties, and Joseph and I had only been married for two months. Coleman and Janny were walking around the reception hall holding hands as they thanked their guests for coming and accepted congratulations. Janny looked beautiful. Her gown was traditional, all white, with no train. She wore a very basic veil and carried one white orchid (her favorite flower), instead of a bouquet. Janny's happiness that day was even greater because she had just been offered a job that morning with The Chinson Plastics Corporation as supervisor of their sales department. She would later become head of the entire eastern seaboard. Eventually the newlyweds approached our table.

"Congratulations, man," Joseph stood to shake Coleman's hand and hug Janny. "Thanks, man, now I'm hoping to be as lucky in my marriage as you." We all smiled. "You guys are both lucky. You snatched the last two of a dying breed – smart, beautiful and, last but not least, faithful black women," I said, wrapping my arm around Janny. During my little speech, I noticed that Coleman was looking at me a little differently, almost admiringly. I dismissed it at the time, of course, since he had just married my best friend. "Well, we'd better finish our rounds. I see my mother giving us the evil eye," Janny said as she hugged Joe. "I'll see you guys at the house." Coleman shakes Joe's hand. "I'll see you two back at the house and, again, thanks for introducing me to Janny. If it weren't for you two, this day wouldn't be here," Coleman says. As he hugs me goodbye, he whispers in my ear, "I just hope I married the right one," smiles at me with those misty eyes, gestures goodbye and walks away with Janny to another couple.

Joe and Coleman went to school together. When I met Joseph, the two were roommates. I thought at the time that Joe and I were more compatible, even though I was physically attracted to Coleman. They were both so good-looking. I felt lucky that early on I had a choice between the two of them.

Although Joe and I had been dating for a year, I was still definitely not fully committed, and felt no shame in being flirtatious with whomever I decided was worthy. Although I thought of Coleman as a pretty boy, he was still fine. And he never passed up an opportunity to grab my butt and laugh when Joe wasn't around. When Joe was there, he would just happen to leave his hand on my thigh, and then would squeeze it for what seemed like an eternity when Joe turned his head. At the age of 19, you think the world is about you, and only you.

Joe and Coleman were just as bad. Coleman would do things like catch me in the hallway, brush up against me, and say something like "excuse me, this hallway is so small," with a great big grin on his face. Or, if he wanted to feel my ass, he would say to Joe, "yo, man, did you see this lint on Taylor's pants?" Joe would always say something like, "when she smacks the shit out of you, I don't want to hear about it."

After we were married, Joe would joke about how I'd better not go on a long trip because he might have to look for a girlfriend. But Joe isn't the flirting type. And I had never stepped over the line – until last night. Now everything that happened in the past between Coleman and me has taken on more importance. I want to know what every little comment meant, every little look.

To be honest, I still don't think that any of it meant anything back then. When we were younger and not committed to anyone, I thought Joe was smart, nice, generous, and good-looking – all the things I would look for in a husband. Joe turned out to be my soul mate, but I don't think I ever lost the crush I had on Coleman.

Should I tell my best friend that I willingly kissed her husband?

I hear Joe unlocking the front door and quietly closing it. My ears follow him as he goes down the hall into the kitchen and opens the refrigerator, then comes back down the hall. I hear the soft plunk of his coat being dropped on the bannister as he walks up the stairs. Then I hear him coming up the hallway to our bedroom.

When he enters the room my back is facing the door, so he probably assumes that I'm sleeping. I can hear him taking his pants off, then his shirt, and pouring what sounds like a glass of water. I turn over to see Joe filling up a second glass with champagne.

"What's the occasion?" I question. "I missed you terribly," Joe admits. I tilt my head and raise my eyebrow in suspicion. Joe hands me a glass and climbs into bed. I sit up and take the glass from his hands, still looking at him and wondering what the champagne is really for. "Drink up," Joe says, so I take a sip. While I begin to swallow, he says excitedly, "Brian also promoted me to manager of our Richmond plant!" My eyes open as wide as saucers and I almost spit out what's in my mouth.

All the details begin to pour from Joe's mouth: "I'll get my own sales department, supervise all the technicians, and," he pauses and I can feel myself leaning toward him in suspense, "a $17,000-a-year increase!" We jump up and hug one another, spilling the champagne all over the bed. Then we lay down, kissing, laughing, and finally, making love. I had missed Joseph, but now Coleman is in my head too.

When I step out of the shower, I can hear Joseph in our bedroom playing with the kids. I use my hand to clear the mirror and look at myself. I'm five-foot, five-and-a-half inches tall and 116 pounds, with dark brown eyes and dark brown hair that I've recently been keeping shorter than I had before. I've always been thin and taken care of myself, but even so I've only been content with my outward self, and honest about my inner feelings, in recent years.

Who am I kidding? That kiss meant a lot to me. What was Coleman thinking? This is only the day after, for God's sake! Looking at my naked reflection, I can see exactly what I'm feeling. Somehow, this view allows me to see the truth. I had *allowed* him to kiss me. At first, it was because I wanted him to feel comforted, and then, because I enjoyed it. I didn't want to continue for fear that it might go too far. Back when Joe and Coleman were roommates, my escapades with Coleman had never really gone too far.

The phone rings. I crack the door to listen to Joseph on the phone. It's Coleman. They are talking about getting together today to look at the blueprints. "Hold on, man," Joe says as he depresses the receiver to answer an incoming call. By the tone of his conversation, I can guess who it is. Joe clicks the receiver again. "Listen, Cole, I'll see you when you get here. Taylor's mother is on the other line." Just like I figured. Joe calls, "Taylor, your mom's on the phone."

I pat myself dry enough to slip my robe on and hurry into the room to answer the phone. Joe hands me the phone with one hand as he wraps his other arm around my waist and slides his hand through the slit in my robe, trying his best to cop a feel of my breasts. When I push his hand away, he smiles and pats me on my ass instead.

"Hi, Mom, how are you doing? You and Daddy are where? When did you leave?" My mother tells me that she and my father decided to take a trip to Boston to visit her sister, and that my father is really getting on her nerves. She wishes he would just go back to Virginia so she can enjoy herself (how like my mother to make a long distance call just to tell me how much of a pain in the ass my father is!). I listen as she goes on, telling me how sick her sister is, and that none of the other sisters have made the effort to spend any time with her. She informs me that she'll be back the following Friday, and we say our goodbyes.

My mother and I have not been close since I became an adult, but when I was a child she was the most important person in the world to me. I have a clear memory of a day when we sat together in the kitchen, with me on her lap. I couldn't have been more than six years old. "Do you know how much I love you?" she asked. "How much?" I responded. "This much!" she said, spreading her arms open as wide as she could. The length of her arms seemed endless. I remember thinking 'that's a whole lot!' Now, it's difficult for us to even have a simple conversation. There just isn't much love there anymore. I think my mother was happiest when we as very young children loved her unconditionally, but when we got older and needed things from her as well, that was too much to ask.

Joe has decided to take the girls off my hands this afternoon since I had such a rough day alone with them yesterday. I decide to call Tricie to see what she is up to. She's painting her son Trevor's bedroom, and both her children are at church with her mother. I tell her that I'll stop by. I put on a pair of blue jeans, sneakers and a white Henley button-down shirt.

As I walk through the house to leave, I yell out, "Joe, I'm taking the car!" I know he won't object. He prefers driving the Ford® Explorer we bought this year rather than the Honda® Accord anyway. I guess it's a 'man' thing.

Tricie only lives about four blocks away from me, in the direction of downtown. The area she lives in is known as Jamesville. I haven't lived in Virginia long enough to find out why. It's full of rich white people and all of their adult children, who attend the college nearby. It's the perfect place for Tricie.

Her apartment is on the third floor of a house. It's really a beautiful apartment, with parquet floors, huge bedrooms, and French doors leading to a porch outside her bedroom. Quite nice. As I pull up, I can hear Tricie's music playing; house music, of course! I walk up the winding stairway to her apartment. The door is cracked, so I push it open cautiously and look down the hallway to see her with a baseball cap on, in overalls that were probably white at one time. Paint is splattered all over the place. She has her back turned to me and is bending over to pick up a can of paint. I call to her, but she turns and walks back into Trevor's room with the paint in her hand.

I shut the door and walked down the hall to the bedroom to find her painting the windowsill and bouncing to the music. "TRESE!" She turns around with a jerk, smiles and walks over to give me a hug. I hold both my hands out to stop her, saying, "No, thanks." She smiles at me, "How long have you been standing there?"

"Not long, I just got here. When are Trevor and Maya coming home?" I ask. "My mother took them to church and then they're supposed to be going to the zoo," Tricie answers, putting the paintbrush into a jar filled with clear water.

"So, what did you do last night?" Tricie asks. I look at her, surprised and wondering why she's asking. "Nothing, why?" "I called Janny to see what you guys were doing, and she said that you and Coleman had gone to get something to eat," she says. I'm relieved – she really only wants to know what I did in general last night, not what I 'did' with Coleman. "She told me she was working on some paper and wanted to finish it," Tricie says.

"Yeah, we went to Rizzario's. I finally tried the Fettuccini Alfredo," I say. "You and Coleman went alone? I didn't have anything to do last night. I could have gone with you guys," she says disappointingly as she heads for the kitchen. "You want a beer?" she yells. "Yes, I'll take one."

Tricie brings back two cold beers. "I used to have such a crush on Coleman," she says. "Really?" I say, surprised. "Oh, yeah!" Tricie assures me as we sit down on the floor. "I love big, tall men, of course, and his complexion was a plus! And those eyes! Mm, mm, mm, he's a killer! It's a good thing that he and Janny are so cute together," she says.

They are indeed, and I'm going to have to use every bit of strength I have to fight the feelings I'm having for Coleman. I don't want to fall in love with him; I love my best friend too much.

"What are you and Joseph doing tonight?" Tricie asks. "Nothing," I answer. "Maybe Andrew and I will stop by. Do you want me to pick up a tape?" I think for a moment. "Yeah, get

'Posse,'" I say. "You never saw that?" she asks. "No, but please don't ever mention it to the press!" We laugh.

I stay and talk with Tricie a little longer and then go home to cook dinner. I try to make sure that Sunday dinner is a little more special than any other day of the week. I have more fun cooking a meal when I don't have a guest list – the pressure is off.

Tricie and her new boyfriend do come over after dinner. Joe and I now have the chance to get to know Andrew a little better. He comes from a very wealthy family, and I'm not happy to find out that Tricie still hasn't met any of them. I don't want him playing out his wildest fantasies with my friend when I know she's putting her heart into this relationship.

Andrew also mentions the fact that he has never dated outside his own race before. Maybe we black women are more opinionated about interracial relationships than our male counterparts, but I just don't dig it. I've been willing to grin and bear it for Tricie's sake, but I have a really big problem with these two as a couple. Both of them are claiming to be in love, but I know for a fact that Tricie is very much aware of the color of his skin before anything else, and I happen to think that Andrew is equally focused on that characteristic. He also mentions in the course of the conversation that he doesn't want children. Tricie jokingly says, "Neither do I." We make light of his revelation, but I know that in a few weeks we'll all be helping Tricie pick up the pieces of her life again.

"What did you think of Andrew?" Joe asks me, sitting in the chair as I put my nightshirt on. "I don't," I answer. "I ask because I just can't understand what Tricie sees in him except the fact that he's white," Joe says. "That's all she sees, I say. "Frankly, I'm tired of always discussing Tricie's love life."

Joe goes into the bathroom and I climb into bed. "Are you going to drive me to the airport next week?" he asks as he re-enters the room. "I didn't know you were still going," I say. "Of course I still have to go, Taylor. You've known about this trip for over a month now," Joe says. "I know, but I just thought with the promotion and all, they might send someone else down instead of you," I explain. "Actually, I'm bringing someone else down with me. His name is William, and he's going to be my replacement," Joe explains.

I really don't care who's going with him or why; the issue is that Joe still has to go. I don't like it when he's gone. Whenever Joseph goes away, it's always for weeks at a time. Luckily, this trip to Atlanta is only for a week.

The phone rings. "Hello," I answer. It's Janny. "Hey, girl, what's going on?" I ask. "Nothing much, but I just remembered that I'm going out of town to Chicago. I'm leaving Sunday morning. Will you get Jolie off to school for me?" Janny asks. "Of course," I say. "When are you coming back?" "I'm not sure; hopefully, by the 30th," she says. "I'm doing some training seminars because the plants are really slacking off down there. What are you doing tomorrow morning?" she asks. "Dawn has gymnastics at ten o'clock, why?" I respond. "I'll meet you over there. I have something to talk to you about," Janny says. We hang up.

What's on her mind? I know Janny well. She doesn't like to discuss things unless it's really a problem. I'll bet it's about work. I'm not going to sleep well tonight.

Monday morning, I successfully get my children off to school and Joseph off to work. By the time I get back home and straighten up the morning mess, I have about 40 minutes to spare, so I do a little reading. On the way to pick up Dawn, I stop at the record store to pick up a few CD's (rap, of course! I'm probably the biggest hip-hop junkie that lives).

About five minutes after I sit down in the parent waiting area of Tumbles and Turnovers Gymnastics, in walks Janny. She has her hair, which she has recently grown long, pulled back tightly in a bun, and is wearing her plain navy blue suit. She has a very serious look on her face, and her eyes are red and puffy. I know she's been crying, and I'm terrified of what she's going to say.

"Hey, girl," she sits beside me looking cautiously into my eyes, "I know you would never lie to me, right?" She grabs hold of my hands, and I can feel the tears welling up in my eyes. "I'm pregnant." I am shocked. She goes on; "Coleman wants me to have a baby so badly, but I can't right now, Taylor, I just can't. I'm going to have an abortion while I'm in Chicago. Do you think I should tell him?"

I take a very deep breath and search for the words to say. "Janny, you know how I feel about abortion. You know that I'm against it one hundred percent. Coleman would freak if he found out what you're planning to do."

"I knew you were going to say that," Janny admits. "Then why did you ask me?" I ask her. "I... I just needed to be reminded of what a big mistake I'm getting ready to make. I've got this conference coming up later this year. I might end up heading the company, Taylor! I'll be the first black woman to do this. There's just no room for a baby," she explains.

I shake my head in amazement, "That's what this is all about, Janny? This baby inside you isn't worth as much as your job? This baby might get in the way of your advancement, so you just want to get rid of it?"

"It's not just that, Taylor. I... I don't want a baby. I don't want... *his* baby." There is a long silence between us. "Why?" I ask. "I think some people just weren't supposed to be married, Taylor. I'm sorry to say that it's taken a great career and years of marriage to find this out, but sometimes I think to myself that things might be better if I was all alone," she says sadly. "What about Jolie?" I say. "I love her, Taylor, she has changed my life for the better. But the way my career has taken off and with all the time I spend at work, I think she and her father would be better off without me. Sometimes I really feel like that."

"You're not thinking about divorce, are you?" I asked. "No way," she says. "I can only handle one thing at a time, and the top thing on my list of priorities is terminating this pregnancy." She hugs me tightly and begins to cry again, "I know you don't agree with me, Taylor, but just give me your blessing, will you?" She pulls away from me, "I love you, Taylor. I wish the love I had for Coleman was like the kind of love you have for Joseph, but not everyone's marriage is that simple."

If she only knew... I am working very hard to keep my marriage what it is, and I do have doubts at times. But I'm not ready to make decisions like that. She is being so brave – much more brave than I could ever be. She will always have my blessing.

Early in the morning on Wednesday, March 23rd, I drive my husband to the airport. I try my best to fight back tears as I watch his plane take off. It reminds me of when I was younger and my father went away. Although my mother was still there, I felt like the foundation of the house was gone. In the same way, things aren't stable when Joe is gone.

I also know that I will have to face Coleman again. I've been avoiding him, and I think he's been avoiding me too. This will give me the opportunity to tell him that I'm sorry for allowing him to kiss me and that I have no feelings for him whatsoever. I need to tell him this so I can put it all behind me.

I arrive back at the house a little late. The girls need to be at school at eight o'clock, and it's now 7:56. Coleman's car is parked in front of the house. I pull up alongside him saying, "I'm so sorry, Coleman, I got caught up in traffic." "That's okay, I'm late myself. What time do you want me to pick her up?" he asks. "I'll give you a call," I answer. We go our separate ways.

My plan is to talk to him about that kiss when I call him. My day is pretty busy. Joe Jr. needs some new shoes, then the kids want to see "The Lion King" for the fifth time, so dinner ends up being McDonald's. By the time we get home, it's well past 8:30 and I know Janny doesn't like Jolie to be up and about past 9:00, so I just let her take a bubble bath with the girls and put her to bed. I'm sure Coleman won't mind.

The house quiets down once the kids are sleeping. I pick up the telephone receiver and hold it in my hand for a moment. All day I've been rehearsing what I'm going to say to Coleman, and now that the time has come, I'm afraid. I don't know how he'll react. Fuck it, I dial his number.

"Hello, Coleman." "Hey, Taylor, are you ready for me to come and get Jolie?" he asks. "No. It was getting so late I thought I would just let her stay the night. Is that okay?" I say. "Yeah, I'll just bring some clothes by in the morning," he replies. "Thanks. Listen, Coleman, I want to talk to you about something..."

There is a dead calm between us. "I want to apologize for that kiss we had the last time we were together. I don't know why I didn't stop you, but I just can't let that happen again. I love Janny too much, I love Joseph too much..."

He interrupts, "Taylor, I should be the one apologizing. I came on to you. It won't happen again; I promise you that. I hope we can still be friends like before." "Of course we'll be friends, Coleman, it was just a kiss!" I replied. "I know, huh?" We laugh, then talk about what I did with the kids today. I'm glad that I talked to him about it. At least now I know that I put a stop to this nonsense. We can go on.

At 3:34 in the morning, I'm awakened by a crack of thunder and a knock on the door. Not quite sure what I'm hearing, I wait. Again, there is a knock at the door. I throw on a robe and hurry downstairs. I look through the peephole; it's Coleman, standing in the rain in nothing but a T-shirt and a pair of jeans. His glasses are wet from the rain. I pull the door open. "Can I come in, Taylor?" he asks. "Of course, Coleman. What are you doing out this late?" I ask. "I have to see you, Taylor." He comes into the foyer, soaking wet, and I hand him a towel from the bathroom. "I've been up thinking ever since you called. I understood everything you said, Taylor. Believe me. I listened to you, but I need to come clean with you, too." I look away, fearful of what he's going to say. "I've been holding back these feelings for a long time, Taylor. When you held me that day, kissing you just seemed right," he says. I back away instinctively. "Do you know how difficult it is to go to bed every night and wonder if you're in bed with the right woman?" "What are you saying, Coleman?" I ask. "I love my wife, or, maybe I should say I've grown to love my wife, but sometimes I think we don't want the same things in life," he responds.

"I can't do this," I interrupt. "Why?" he asks. "Because I'm afraid," I answer. "Of what, Taylor?" he pleads. "I'm afraid that I won't be able to stop this time," I admit. Coleman walks up to me and pulls me to him. I can feel his damp clothes through my robe. He lifts my chin up with his fingers, then runs his hand down the side of my neck and pushes my hair away from my face. "I can't walk away from you anymore, Taylor. I need to be with you." He presses his mouth against mine, his lips tasting salty from the mixture of rain and perspiration. I take his glasses from his face and wrap both my arms around his neck.

Coleman says quietly, "I didn't come this far to be turned away again." We kiss without hesitation and begin to do what we have both wanted ever since the night we kissed. Coleman lifts me up, carries me to the living room and stands me in front of the fireplace. I glance down to watch as he slowly unties my robe. I'm acutely aware of his towering physique so close to me. He runs his hands under my nightshirt and against my bare waist, pushes my robe off my shoulders and plants tender kisses on my collarbone. I push down on his shoulders, directing him down to kiss across my stomach. As he kneels down, I drape my bare leg over his shoulder. Coleman takes the cue and faintly kisses around the outside of my panties, teasingly sticking his finger underneath and letting it rub gently against my labia while kissing and biting at my panties all the while. I am melting. Standing up again, he commands my mouth and begins to thrust his tongue in and out, running his hands over my ass and up my back. I bite his bottom lip in excitement. With one quick effort he lifts me up, taking a mouthful of my tit. I wrap my legs around his waist, freeing his hands to undo his pants. I rip his shirt open, popping off a few buttons as his large hands come back to caress my ass. The hair on his chest feels cold, curling up between my fingers.

He lies down in front of the fireplace, adjusting me on top of him and kicking off his pants. Now, with us both disrobed, I can enjoy him in all his glory. Truth be told, I had always imagined fucking him like this: his legs spreading mine apart, his tight stomach up against mine, his long limbs not letting any of me remain untouched. He continues to kiss and fondle me, sitting up partway and pulling me up to his mouth. At times he rolls me over to lunge his tongue deep inside me and take delicate mouthfuls of my clit, rotating his tongue slowly around it until he senses my impending orgasm and pulls away.

Just as I think my pleasure can't get any more intense, he enters me with a strenuous shove, then with raw passion he pulls back and forces his dick into me again with more force than the first time. Feeling restricted, he stands me up in front of him with his body pressed against mine and begins to fuck me from behind, pulling on my hips to meet his every blow, driving harder and harder. I can feel myself slipping into ecstasy. With rhythmic thrusts, the two of us climax harmoniously. His muscles twitch as his body jerks with pleasure.

Coleman turns me around to hold me tightly. Knowing what we have just done, I begin to cry. I'm glad to have finally been able to express my love for him and, even better, to confirm that he feels the same as I do. But as we cuddle on the couch, with our wet bodies pressed up against one another and breathing heavily, I realize the magnitude of what we have just done. All night long, we make love in the guest room between my tears. Each time I cry, he consoles me. We both know why I'm crying and there is nothing we can say.

I wake up at 6:30 the next morning, startled because I know I've slept late. Bailey, Dawn and Jolie have to be at school by 8:00 and Joe Jr. has to be at daycare between 8:15 and 8:45. I don't awaken Coleman. I know he'll know where I'm going. Before leaving, I look back at him. He's lying on his back with both his arms above his head and the sheet just barely draped over his midsection. When I return home, I'm hoping to find him right where I left him. As I enter the room he is just coming out of the guest bath with his jeans undone, no shirt and bare feet. It embarrasses me to see another man like this in my house. Sure, Coleman and I were intimate last night, but that was sudden and visceral. This was somehow more personal.

"Are you bothered by me being here like this?" he asks. I smile and reply, "A little." "Taylor, I didn't come over here last night just to screw you," Coleman explains, winking at me. "In my mind, I had done that already. I came here because I couldn't wait any longer. I needed to be near you.

"It started when I was talking to Janny before she left and she was telling me that she just doesn't want any more children. I was trying to push her to have more kids. That's when it hit me that I was trying to create the kind of family *I* wanted.

"I remember back in 1990 when Joe brought you back to the dormitory for the first time with your cute little ass. I said to myself, 'yo, I want to git wit dat.' I didn't care what Joe thought. I thought you were so cute. I was going to grab you and stick my tongue in your ear every chance I got." We smile and he continues, "Initially, I was just physically attracted to you. Joe told me that you didn't like banana boys but I didn't pay any attention to that. As time went on, I started to have more intense feelings for you. It wasn't enough just seeing your smile and hearing your voice. I wanted to hold you, touch you. Shit, I wanted you to be my girl." Coleman buckles his belt. "It got to the point where whenever I knew that Joe was bringing you over to the crib, I spent more time in the mirror than he did. Man, I would fuck with Joe just before he left and hope that you two would have a messed-up date." In one continuous movement he reaches for me, sits down on the bed and pulls me onto his lap. "I think I'm in love with you and I can't keep going on like this. Damn, girl." He squeezes my arms, "I want you."

"I used to flirt with you, too," I admit. "I let you grab my ass. I let you kiss me a little longer, even though Joe was there. But why this revelation now?"

"Taylor, after all this time, I'm telling you how I feel because I think you may feel the same for me. I can't give you away again. Do you want me, too?" I look him in the eyes. "Yes, I do." I can see joy and sadness in his eyes. "You need to know that I won't just sneak around with you, Taylor. I have too much respect for my family and Joseph to do that," he says. "So what are we supposed to do?" I ask. "I guess we need to take some time and think about what we want. When that time is up, we'll either decide to be together or go our separate ways." He lays me down, caressing my face and looking me over. "I'm supposed to be here with you," he says. We kiss, holding each other tightly and feeling the closeness we never expressed before. Years ago I thought I was just being flirtatious with a tall, muscular, hazel-eyed, cream-colored model-type boy. Now, I can see that he is a sensitive, caring, devoted family man (with a really cute butt and muscled abdomen to go with the package). Now it's serious. We are in love.

7 DECEIT ALL AROUND

During the next week, Coleman and I spend a lot of time at Jefferson Lake together, finding out just how much we have in common. I tell him about how I would purposely disconnect the telephone whenever he was talking to another girl, and how I would just happen to walk into the bathroom at the dormitory when he was getting out of the shower. We hold hands and cuddle like a couple who have been separated for years. In a sense, we were just that.

During that week, we also conclude that we need to be together. It is right, so right. I don't know how I could have mistaken my love for Joseph, but I now know that part of this empty feeling I have inside me is beginning to fill up. I just don't know what I'm going to do with this love I have for Joseph and my children. I feel guilty. And Joseph will be home the day after tomorrow.

Coleman and I break our very first promise to each other. When Joseph and Janny return, we don't tell either of them what we want. We don't admit our love for one another. We continue living a charade. The charade goes on from winter, through spring and into summer, and past my son's first birthday. It continues as my husband becomes manager of the Richmond-based chemical control plant and as Janny becomes the first black female to be named president of Chinson Plastics, Inc. We have lived this lie for the past six months.

Even worse, we do exactly what Coleman never wanted to do - meet in discreet places and whisper "I love you" in hushed voices on the telephone. I am ashamed of what I've become. I'm so angry with myself for being deceitful with my husband and children, yet I can't stop. Joseph is one of the best things that's ever happened to me. He is my knight in shining armor because he walked me across the threshold into a normal, loving lifestyle. This was everything I wanted as a child. And I now I'm destroying it.

I had hoped that I would never make the decisions my father did. I knew about my father's affairs. Sadly, my mother was the first to tell me about them.

When my parents were first married, they were members of the social elite. My mother was a former model. My father was a handsome young doctor. They looked like the perfect couple. My mother never drank until she married my father and began to drink socially. She told me that her first drink made her sick. She was so embarrassed because all the other women looked so sophisticated in their silk gowns and expensive jewelry, holding champagne flutes in their hands, and she couldn't even keep a rum and Coke down. When she saw how important it was to my father that she dressed and acted the part, she began to throw parties at the house.

This was also the time when she began to notice my father's roaming eye, lengthy kisses at parties, and long nights out with "the boys." My mother began to drink alone. She would drink whenever my father wasn't home, often to the point of passing out. When my father came home and found her intoxicated, he would leave again to find a woman who wasn't drunk. My mother's drinking habit also caused depression, weight gain, and very low self-esteem, which just gave my father more reasons to go out and find women who were outgoing, thin and self-assured.

At one point, Mom packed my brothers, my sister, and me up and moved us to her mother's house in New Jersey. This took some courage, but the bravest thing my mother did was admit that she had a drinking problem and get help. And she was successful. She finally announced to my father that there would only be one woman in his life, and with good behavior, it might be her. Needless to say, he changed his ways.

When I became a teenager, I asked my father if these things ever happened, and his response was, "I never did anything in front of your mother." He also told me that he had his suspicions about my mother sleeping with one of their friends. Whatever the case, my parents didn't exactly show me how to have a healthy monogamous relationship. My mother wanted a stable father for her children, unlike her own father and many stepfathers. She was willing to sacrifice her pride and her own personal goals for a while. However, I think she wishes she had followed through with the things that were important to her, (like finishing school) and that she had borne children later in life.

My mother has become a bitter person. Her grudge against my father has intensified over the years, while surprisingly, my father has learned to love my mother for the qualities she used to have. He often talks about how smart and beautiful my mom was. He'll also say that he's in it for the long haul; perhaps this is from guilt. Whatever the case may be, they have come full circle, although their circles are separate rather than interlocked.

Isn't it ironic that I have now interlocked my circle with *two* men: one I love with all my heart and soul, and the other gives me love I'm afraid to live without.

While getting my children ready for summer camp one morning, I pick up the phone to call Daneka. It's been a while since I talked to her and I'm looking forward to our conversation. "Hello, Daneka Smith, please," I request. She soon answers the call. I ask her if her schedule is open this morning; I'm hoping to have an early lunch with her. She agrees.

I drop the girls off at school and Joe Jr. at daycare. On the way to Daneka's office, I think about how I first met her. She worked in the Patient Admissions Department at Deston Memorial Hospital, the hospital where I delivered Bailey. When Joseph and I came in, I was in a lot of pain. This was our first experience in a hospital and we were confused, anxious and not up for much conversation. Daneka had her braids pulled back into a neat corn roll and was a whiz at her job, even then. She kept promising Joseph and me that things would go very smoothly, despite the fact that Joseph had left all of our insurance information at the house. I remember thinking that she looked so pretty and I was just this fat thing with a baby about to burst out of my stomach.

I take the elevator to the 27th floor and look for Suite 2740, "La Negra, Inc." This is Daneka's dream job, writing and doing research for one of the most popular black-owned magazines in the world. As I enter the glass doorway to Suite 2740, Daneka is standing at the front desk, conversing with one of the magazine's editors. She sees me enter and waves. "Hi, Taylor, let me go grab my jacket." I watch her go to her office and grab her jacket off the back of her chair. "Let's go downstairs," she suggests, "the food in our cafeteria is really good." I put my arm around her shoulder and we enjoy small talk on the way down.

Daneka is much shorter than I am, and is what most black men would call "healthy," which means she has a voluptuous figure. Today she wears her braids straight down, falling just below her earlobes, and has on a pair of little round black eyeglasses. She is wearing a short-sleeved, fitted full-length brown dress, accented only by a leather woven tasseled belt that is wrapped around her waist.

Daneka doesn't date very often. This is not because there aren't many men asking – very handsome, intelligent men are always approaching her. It's because Daneka doesn't want to get married. She enjoys being with men, but has often joked that she will only marry a man who is willing to wear the skirt so she can wear the pants!

"So, what's new?" I ask. Daneka looks at me with a great big grin on her face. "Well, I think I've just about got South Africa in the bag!" she exclaims. We hug. "When did you find out? How soon will you know?" I ask. "Wait until you hear this one," Daneka says, setting the story up. "*Shirley* told Jason, my senior editor, that she thought it was about time *I* take on a project like this!" "How long is the assignment for?" I ask. Daneka lifts her soda to her mouth, takes a long drink and folds her hands in front of her. "Six and a half months."

My mouth opens wide enough to hit the table. I just stare at her with a shocked look on my face, shaking my head from side to side. "Daneka, why so long?" I ask. "Well, that leads me to the other good news," she responds. "Why is it that I don't think it's going to be that good?" I say. "If I want, La Negra is going to pay for me to study at the University," she says. "How long will you be over there?" I ask. "About three years." A loud crash comes from the kitchen that is perfectly timed to distract me from crying. I'm so very proud of Daneka, but I don't like it when my friends are so far away from me. I know she's aware of how I feel about things like this, which is probably why she decided to tell me first, alone. She also knows that I would never let my feelings get in the way of what I thought was best for her, and this is certainly what is best for her. Daneka has wanted to get to this point in her career for a long time, and it's about time.

"So, when are you going to tell Janny and Tricie?" I asked. "Probably this weekend. I was thinking that we should take Janny out for her birthday..." I interrupt, "Shit! I almost forgot Janny's birthday! I've got to do something!" "We should take her out to a club," Daneka suggests, "girls only!" "That sounds good. Call me tomorrow and we'll get something together," I say. I gather my coat to get ready to leave as I ask her, "Daneka, do you ever think about having children and a family?" "No, not really. That's just not me right now. I don't need a man to define me and I surely don't need a child to limit me! I'm not cut out for that. I'll leave that stuff up to you guys," she says. I smile and turn to walk away.

"Taylor!" I turn around. Daneka walks up to me and says, "My birth mother abandoned me when I was three days old. She left me on the church steps. I just found that out three years ago and, needless to say, it devastated me. I'm not over it yet. Until I can mend that hole in my life, I can't invite anyone else into it." "Were you ready to tell me that?" I question. "Not really, but I'm glad it's over. I didn't know how to bring it up," she answers. "I've got to go, I'm running late. We'll talk more later." I gesture goodbye and say, "Don't forget to call me about Janny's get-together."

I leave to run errands. I'm thinking about asking Coleman if he wants to meet for a late lunch, but am unable to get in touch with him. Whenever I want to talk to him, I page him. Coleman knows if it's a page from me, it means that I have time to spend with him.

I'm not proud of my current relationship with Coleman. We haven't had sex since that night in my house seven months earlier, but we don't need sex to keep us together. We know that we love each other for who we were years ago, and who we are now. The sex part, until that night, was the only unexplored territory.

The thing that frightens me the most about being with Coleman is how my love for him keeps growing stronger as I learn more about him. I love his passion for his work, his love of poetry, and the way he gives everything that is dear to him one hundred percent of his effort, even his marriage. I can't deny myself the possibility of total happiness anymore. But I can't figure how to leave Joseph, either.

Whether I like it or not, I have fallen in love with my husband, but in a different way. I love the *idea* of being in love with Joseph. He is a man, in every sense of the word. His ability to take control of his life is one of the things that drew me to him at the beginning. I hoped that some of his take-charge confidence would rub off on me. In those days I was terrified of having to deal with challenges and issues, but Joe was able to handle any obstacle, even if he was afraid. He is a born leader, whereas I had to practice to become one.

When I walk in the front door that evening, I see Bailey sitting at the computer. Joseph is sitting on the couch. Joe Jr. is sitting by Joseph's feet with his eyes glued to the fire burning in the fireplace, playing with one of his toy trucks. Dawn has conveniently fallen asleep on the floor with her doll in her hand. "Hey, Baby, can you throw this away for me?" he asks as he holds out an empty beer can. I walk over to him and kiss him, taking the can from his hand. "Did they eat?" "Of course, my dear. You're not the only one skilled in the kitchen," he answers.

I turn to walk down the hallway to the kitchen and meet Coleman halfway there. Surprised, I almost drop the beer can. "What are you doing here? Did you get my page?" I whisper. "I've been here," he answers quietly. "I didn't want to keep avoiding Joe. I want to see you tomorrow," he whispers while steadying the can in my hands. "I'll call you at 8:15 after I get back from dropping the girls off at school," I say. Coleman kisses me lightly so that we can't be overheard, neither one of us wanting to let go, but realizing we must.

I can hear Coleman telling Joseph he needs to leave. After a little small talk between them, Joe walks him to the door. Hoping to avoid Joe immediately after their exchange, I begin to wash the dishes. Joe comes into the kitchen and grabs my waist from behind. "There's one thing that I've always loved about you, Taylor," he says. "What's that, baby?" He turns me around to face him and says, "I could always read your emotions, because they're written all over your face." I try to act ignorant; "Really?" Joe looks at every part of my face, except into my eyes. I can tell he doesn't want to look too deep for fear he might see something he doesn't want to know. "Can you see how much I love you in these scriptures on my face?" he asks. "Always," I respond. He kisses me on the forehead, like he does when he's leaving. I lean against the sink and watch him walk down the hall. I turn back around to finish the dishes and call out, "Do you want me to get them ready for their baths?" He answers, "No, I got it," just before going upstairs. I'm thinking about Coleman too much to go straight to bed, so I decide to work on the children's journals and wait for Daneka to call.

This is one of the only times in our marriage when I'm hoping he'll be asleep before I come to bed. While I'm writing in Joe Jr.'s journal, the phone rings. It's Daneka. We begin to plan Janny's party, and decide to take her to some of the clubs in Washington, DC since Virginia doesn't have many "hopping" clubs. We want to go out, drink heavily, and just be girls again for 24 hours. The plan is to kidnap her from work late Friday evening.

"You know what would be good? We should have her clothes already packed. That way she can't wear one of those boring-ass suits," Daneka suggests. "Okay, I'll go by her house Friday morning and get some of her things," I answer, thinking about her as my best friend rather than my lover's wife. "I will also pick up Tricie and we'll meet you in the lobby of Janny's building."

After talking to Daneka, I decide to go upstairs to bed. It's now 10:45 and all the lights are off. I can smell baby lotion and powder as I near the top of the stairs. I can also hear Bailey snoring (she gets that from her mother). Our bedroom light is also off, so I tiptoe into our bathroom to wash my face and put on my nightshirt, making sure to turn the bathroom light off before opening the door. I climb into bed and snuggle up close to Joe. By now the bed is nice and warm from his body heat. I begin to relax, thinking he is asleep.

"Who was that on the phone?" Joe asks. "Daneka. We're going to take Janny to Washington Friday night for her birthday. Will you be here to watch the kids?" I ask. "Yes. You know she's not going to like the idea of being so far away from her laptop," Joe says. "I know," I answer, "but she's going to have to learn for at least one night." I kiss him on the back of his neck, wrapping my arms around his body and holding onto his chest. "Goodnight, baby," I say. "'Nite, love," he responds.

Just as I'm about to fall asleep, the phone rings. I look at the clock to make sure it really is as late as I think. It's 11:49 p.m. "Hello?" I answer. "Hey, Taylor, what's up?" Recognizing his voice, I say, "Adam?" "Yeah, what are you doing?" he asks. "The same thing most people with children are doing at 11:49 at night. What's up?" I say sarcastically, rolling over and trying not to wake Joseph.

"Nothing. I just finished talking to Deandra and she reminded me that I don't talk to my family enough. How's Mommy?" he asks. "Okay, I guess. She and Daddy went to Boston back in March and you know she called me to rag on Daddy. I don't know why she insists on doing that," I say. "You know Mommy. Anyway, I'm going to be in town this weekend. What are you and Joe doing?" he asks. "Nothing, we'll be here... oh, shit!... What day are you coming?" I ask. "Saturday morning," he says. "Good, because Friday night we're taking Janny out of town for her birthday, but I'll be back Saturday morning." "Is Joe up?" Adam asks. "No, he's asleep. Do you want me to wake him?" I ask. "Naw, tell him I'll get with him this weekend. I'll talk to you later, Taylor." "Bye, Adam."

My brother lives in New York City and is an engineer for a major oil company. He is dating a girl named Tammy, who lives in Spotsylvania County, Virginia. They've been together for the past two years, which is a record for Adam. He doesn't exactly have a good history with women because he has shied away from commitment.

Even though I've only met Tammy once, I know that my brother loves her very much. I think they're perfect for each other in the sense that they both seem to handle the long-distance relationship well. My brother is also learning to get a handle on his control issues. In his case, it's not about needing to control others, it's about his belief that everyone is always trying to control *him*. He can't stand the idea of people telling him what to do or how to do it. Our mother did that for the first 18 years of his life, and I have watched him go in and out of many relationships over that issue alone. However, commitment and family have really begun to appeal to him since Joe and I got married. He's also become more interested in having children since he has been around our babies.

Tuesday morning, I wake up and decide to take the kids to my mother's house for a visit, which is a chore. I hate going to my mother's house because our conversations are so forced. But she loves her grandchildren in her own way, and they think she hangs the moon and stars.

As I pull up the driveway, Bailey looks up and notices where we are. "Oooooh, Grandma's! Are we going to stay the night?" she asks. "I don't think so, sweetie. We are just going to visit for a little while," I answer, not really wanting to stay too long.

I don't like the way I feel about my mother. I want to have a storybook relationship with her, and as a small child I had that. But once I was older and needed more from her, the bond disintegrated. I've finally learned to accept that it's too late for her to change, but it's not too late for me to be the best daughter I can be. It's no longer about what I want, as long as my children are getting what they need from their grandmother. This takes precedence over my feelings.

"Can I ring the bell, Mommy?" Dawn asks, reaching for the doorbell. "Go ahead, puddin." I lift Joe Jr. up to the window at the top of the door so that she can see his precious little face when she answers our ring. I can hear her voice faintly saying, "Oh, look at this little man!" My mother pulls the door open and Bailey and Dawn spill into the entryway, grabbing her legs. "Grandma!" they yell. "How arc you doing, Mom?" I ask, kissing her on the cheek. "I'm doing fine, how have you been?" she answers, rubbing my arm.

I can't help but notice that the house reeks of cigarette smoke. My mom smokes at least two packs a day. She sits down and places all three kids on and around her lap and begins to take off their sweaters. Bailey starts to tell her about the things she's been doing at camp, and Dawn repeats every word as if it's her own. Joe Jr. is itching to get down from her lap. "He's been walking," I brag. "Getting out of the way for another one, huh?" she questions. "Not in the Wayland household," I promise.

"Mom, can I leave them here for a little bit?" I ask. I've got a few things to do." "Of course," she says. "Your father will be here soon and I know he will want to see them. Do you want me to give them dinner?" I look at my watch. It's only 12:36 p.m. I think to myself, 'maybe I can spend the whole day with Coleman.' "Yes, I think I'll take you up on that." Before I leave I page Coleman and he calls right back. "I'll get that, Mom, it's for me. Hello?" I answer. "Wassup?" Coleman asks. "Nothing, where do you want to meet?" I ask. "Meet me downtown in front of Jason's," he answers. "See you in a little bit," I hang up the phone. I walk over to my mother and kiss her on the cheek. "I'm going to go." I also kiss Bailey, Dawn, and Joe Jr.. None of them cry because they love being at Grandma's. "See you later!" I wave goodbye and get into the car, heading toward downtown.

When I arrive at Jason's, I park my car and walk around to the front of the store to wait for Coleman. He is always on time, and I have a habit of being late. We hadn't set a time when we spoke, so this time I am probably very early.

I glance down at my clothes to make sure I look okay. I'm wearing a white V-neck bodysuit and a pair of white shorts with a drawstring at the waist. When I look up, I see Coleman driving up. He's in his Volvo 960 today. I smile at him and get into his car, and we drive off.

Soon he pulls the car over and puts it in park, leans over, places his hand in mine and kisses me. I love it when he leaves his five o'clock shadow. Janny hates it. Feeling his scratchy whiskers lets me know that I have the upper hand today. He's wearing a black baseball cap, a pair of shades, a navy blue, black and white striped shirt with a pair of white shorts, and sandals with no socks. His legs are just hairy enough, and muscular. Coleman runs 10 miles every morning, and it shows.

"You look good, girl. I've missed you," Coleman confesses. "You, too. What's going on?" I ask. "Nothing really. Janny has been spending most of her days and evenings at Chinson, as you already know," he says. "I know," I answer. "Whenever she's gone, I long for you, Taylor. We need to make a move," he pleads. "I know," I admit. "It's become difficult lying to Joseph. It's not that we have that much to hide as far as intimacy goes, but I hate the idea of lying to him when I tell him I love only him."

"Taylor, I've told you before that it's up to you. My marriage has become a marriage of convenience. All you have to do is say the word and we can do this together. I want to be with you. I can't stand not being able to make love with the woman I love," he says. "I can't just set a date," I say. "Why not?" he argues. "I can't be that selfish about it," I answer. "By not setting a date, that's exactly what you're doing. What about my feelings, Taylor? What about your feelings?"

Coleman is upset. He faces me, removes his shades and pulls the drawstring to my shorts loose. "I need to feel you, Taylor, I can't stand being away from you," he says as he pulls me closer to him, pressing his mouth against mine, first sucking on my bottom lip then opening his mouth and rolling his tongue across mine. He's a good kisser and always holds me tight. I can tell he wants to slide his hand inside my shirt, but we made a pact that he would not touch my bare body again until we are together as a couple. I'm having trouble holding my hands back too. While kissing him, I run my hands through his curly hair, not letting him move away from me. Finally, he runs his hand up the side of my shorts, just high enough to reach my underwear. He then moves his mouth and begins to skim his wet tongue down my neck, then runs his hand across my chest. Coleman rests his forehead on my chest while I hold his head against me. "I want you to have my children, Taylor," he looks at me, almost pouting. "I want to have your children, too, Coleman, so let's take care of this soon," I respond as he kisses me. I just want to make sure I'm making the right decision. My heart says I am.

We leave our parking spot, drive around a little while longer, and then enjoy a late lunch together. Whenever we're together it feels like puppy love. We feed each other, wipe each other's mouths, and nibble on each other's ears. Absolutely every touch gives me exquisite tingles all over my body. When we finish our meal, we share a glass of wine.

"I'm going to tell Joe this summer," I announce. "Are you serious?" Coleman asks, surprised to hear me say that out of the blue. "The thing that's been so hard for me is that I love Joseph, and I know he hasn't done anything wrong, except to fall in love with me. I can't stand the thought of betraying him the way that I have," I say as I begin to cry.

Coleman slides closer to me, cradling me in his arms. I continue, "I wanted so badly to believe that the feelings I had for you were just lust, but they're not. I've never felt love the way I feel love for you, Coleman. I just don't understand why love has to cause so much pain." Coleman puts his hand under my chin and lifts my head, saying, "I'm in this with you, Taylor, and we will do this together."

He is so right; we *are* in this together. I've had the opportunity to be loved by two wonderful men, but now I need to let one of them go. This also means I will lose a best friend. But trying to hold onto both is selfish of me and not fair to everyone else involved.

After Coleman drops me off at my car, I pick up the kids from my mother's house and rush home. I like to have dinner cooked by 5:30, in time for Joe when he gets home. It's already 5:15 and I haven't even taken anything out of the freezer yet. "Would you guys like some pizza for dinner?" I ask the kids as we enter the house. "I want Burger King," Dawn announces. "We had dinner at Grandma's," Bailey answers. "That's right, what did she have for you guys?" I ask. "Steak and onions with mashed potatoes and corn. Dawn didn't eat her mashed potatoes because she didn't like them very much," answers Bailey. I bend down to tickle Dawn, "You didn't like them very much?" I tease. Joe comes in the door behind us. "Hi, baby, how was work?" I ask, hugging and kissing him. "Busy, hectic, and busy again. What's for dinner?" he asks. "Whatever can be delivered in 30 minutes or less!" We smile.

The girls take Joe Jr. into the basement to play while Joe and I sit at the table eating pizza. I'm not eating very much since I just ate a late lunch with Coleman. "What did you do today?" Joe asks. "I went to my mother's house for a while," I answer. "How is she doing?" he asks. I shrug my shoulders and roll my eyes upward, "Okay, I guess, I didn't stay for long." Joe looks up from his plate.

"I had to meet with Daneka and talk about our final plans," I say, feeling guilty. "So, what did you decide?" Joe asks. "We are still going to Washington... oh, shit! I forgot to call Raymond and tell him that we're planning on picking Janny up by 4:30 on Friday." "Are you guys staying the weekend?" Joe asks. "No, Adam is coming into town Saturday morning... another thing I forgot to do!" I answer. "What's that?" he asks. "Tell you about Adam," I say.

Joe doesn't seem to mind. He is very good about letting me go away when I need to. He seems to realize how much of a strain it is to be at home with the children every day. It's like being confined to your place of employment. I know he misses me when I'm not here, and I miss him, too, but there are times when the stress levels get so high that I need a little break.

We finish our dinner and put the kids to bed. Joe seems a little different to me, but then again, everything now looks suspicious to me. Somehow, I have a feeling that he knows I'm struggling with something. Joseph is far too observant to miss all the signs I can't help revealing.

That night in bed we talk about the added mental strain he had at work, and how he looked forward to being home with his family. That is classic Joe; he is a genuine family man. I like the way he creates this 'idea' of a family for me. It's something I will never be able to experience again, not in the same way.

Friday morning finally arrives. Joseph has taken the day off so I can tighten up all the loose ends of this surprise we are planning for Janny. I have the house keys from Coleman, so I go by their house while she is at work. I want to pick out something really fun for Janny to wear. I'm convinced that Janny has something hip and cute in her closet, but just chooses not to wear it. To my dismay, there is nothing like that in her house at all. Almost all of Janny's underwear is black or dark brown, and all of her bras are those 'total coverage' types! After spending an hour in her closets and drawers and coming up empty-handed, I decide that my birthday present to her will be some clothes and undergarments that the rest of the twenty-something population enjoys wearing!

I drive to a store called "The Underground" and buy her some really nice tight-fitting jeans, two very colorful T-shirts, and some really cool shoes. I then visit Victoria's Secret and buy her a couple of push-up bras and matching bikini underwear, hoping that this will be just the motivation she needs to get rid of those damned old-lady briefs!

After about an hour or so of shopping for some of Janny's favorite body creams, some birthday balloons, lots of alcohol for the hotel room, and a "Birthday Girl" nightshirt, I use my car phone to call Daneka and make sure she's still on schedule. She answers the phone, "Daneka Smith. May I help you?" "Daneka, it's me, Taylor," I say. "Hey, girl, I'm on time. I won't be late. What time is it anyway?" she asks. I look at my watch. "It's 2:20." "Did you talk to Raymond?" "Yes," I assure her. "Her whole department is going to be ready. He said they'll make sure Janny is in her office."

"What about Tricie? Daneka asks. "I'm going over there now to pick her up. Andrew is keeping the kids, did she tell you?" I ask. "Yeah, I talked to her yesterday. This is a big step for her. She's really scared. I don't know that I'm comfortable with it. I mean, I know they've been together a year now, but you know how I feel about her interracial dating," Daneka finishes. "I don't care what anyone says, I don't like it. It's too soon for Trevor and Maya to be with him alone like that," I say angrily. "Has he been with them overnight?" Daneka asks. "I don't know. I think they're getting pretty serious. She told me that they want to look for an apartment together," I answer. "Listen, I gotta wrap up! I'll see you in about an hour and a half," she says. "I'll meet you in the lobby," I say as we hang up.

I drive toward Demerick's Ballet School, where Beatrice is an instructor. I always enjoy watching Tricie dance. She's been dancing since she was seven years old. I walk into the studio, passing all the ballerinas-to-be. Some are quickly shoving their feet into their slippers, obviously late for class, while others are paired off, sitting in little groups, going over their weekend and talking about their upcoming competitions. All of the classroom's front walls are made of two-way glass, which enables spectators, prospective students, parents, and just plain old nosy people like me to watch classes in session.

When I reach Tricie's studio, I look in to see her finishing up with a class of eight-year olds. I can see her walking along the barre behind the students, correcting their form and posture. She is motioning to the pianist, possibly to have her hurry up and finish. I sit down to watch. Finally, she opens the door and her students hurry out. She comes out behind them and smiles when she sees me. "Hey, do I have time to run home?" she asks. I look at my watch. "I just need to pick up my bags," she says, hurrying by all the people who have crowded the hallways in her pink sleeveless leotard, pink tights, white skirt and ballet slippers. After collecting all of her belongings, she walks over and gives me a hug and a kiss. "Did you watch any of the class?" she asks. "Yes, I've been here for about 30 minutes," I reply, checking my watch again. "It's 3:03, Tricie. We're supposed to meet Daneka at 4:00. What do you need to get?" I ask. "I just need to pick up the bags I packed this morning." "Are you going to change your clothes?" I question, looking down at her skirt. "Well, do I have time? You're the only one rushing me!" she responds. "Yes, as long as you hurry!"

We walk to the car and set out for her apartment. "So... Andrew is watching the kids, huh?" I asked. "Yeah. Daneka told you, huh?" Tricie asks sarcastically. "Yeah, I talked to her on the way here. How do you feel about him being alone with Trevor and Maya?" I ask. "I absolutely don't have a problem with it, Taylor. Why are we even having this conversation?" she demands.

"Because I care about them, Tricie. I want the best for you and I don't know that I'm comfortable with the kids spending the whole night alone with him," I say. Tricie turns around in her seat to face me with a displeased look on her face. She crosses her arms. "You know what, Taylor? You, Janny, and Daneka are my very best friends in the world. Next to my children, I hold you guys the closest in my heart. I may be the baby in this circle, but you all have to let go! If I want your advice, I will ask for it. Damn it, I love you, but Andrew and I are a couple and will make our own decisions!" explodes Tricie.

I'm so angry with Tricie right now. In my heart, I've always wanted her to feel secure enough to make up her own mind and do what she feels is right. After her divorce she needed so much from her friends, and we all adapted to our roles as her providers. Now she is beginning to take back control of her life. As much as I don't agree with her dating Andrew, I need to back off. I love Beatrice, so I decide to do just that.

"I'm sorry, Tricie. I shouldn't have said what I said. I guess I just can't help what I feel," I say as I feel the tears building up in my eyes. I feel guilty about trying to take over her life. To be honest, trying to help people with their lives gives me a sense of control. People consider me a 'well-rounded wife and mother,' and the advice I give is usually pretty good, so friends tend to allow me the right to offer it. But sometimes I take the advising too far.

There is silence in the car between the two of us. When I pull up to the front of Tricie's apartment, she begins to get out of the car, stops, and then turns back to me and says, "Taylor, I'm not angry. I love you so much, but you have to let go. I need to do this on my own." I smile and kiss her on her cheek. "Hurry," I say, pointing at the clock on the dashboard.

Tricie grabs her bags, runs up the front steps, and unlocks her front door. She disappears inside. About 10 minutes later, she returns wearing a pair of denim shorts, a cropped half-shirt, and white scrunched socks and sneakers, and has her hair pulled into a ponytail high on top of her head. She opens the back car door, throws her bags on the seat and jumps into the front seat, chewing and trying to talk at the same time. "What are you eating?" I ask, pulling her hand to me. "Oreos®, you want one?" She opens her hand revealing a fistful of cookies. I take one as we head over to La Negra. When we get there, I park in front of the building, thinking I'll put my hazard lights on and run upstairs. It is now 4:05. When I enter the lobby, Daneka is just getting out of the elevator. "Do you know what time it is? Miss, *I'm* on time," Daneka says as we rush into the car and drive over to Janny's office.

On the way over, we stop to pick up a dozen fresh wild orchids, her favorite flower, and two balloons - one with a "2" on it and the other with a "6" on it - and a bottle of Monet dry wine, also her favorite. When we get to Chinson, everyone in Janny's suite knows what we're there for. They smile and begin to huddle together when we walk in, preparing for the moment of Janny's surprise. Just before we get to her office, with its door strategically closed tight, Raymond walks up to us whispering, "She thinks that Philip from headquarters is coming to take her out to dinner. Whenever Phil comes, she keeps her door closed." "Thanks, Raymond," I say, patting him on his back. "You guys ready?" Raymond asks. We all nod in agreement. Daneka turns to everyone in the office and puts her forefinger to her lips, motioning for everyone to be quiet.

Raymond then rushes in the door, startling Janny. "Janice, Philip is downstairs and he is PISSED! You were supposed to meet with him an hour ago, and he has missed his flight!" Raymond announces. "Dammit, Ray!" Janny stands up flipping the pages in her appointment book, "Shonda told me he'd be here at four o'clock!" Janny grabs her jacket and her purse, hurrying to the door. Just as she exits, we all yell, "SURPRISE!" She drops her purse and leans up against the door jam. We run up to her, hug her, and tell her, "We're taking you away to play for the night!" as we hand her the flowers and balloons. We take turns kissing her cheeks.

Everyone in her office begins to settle back down. They come up to Janny one by one to wish her a happy birthday. Tricie and I take Janny by her hands and start to escort her out the door. She instinctively tries to resist saying, "Just where do you guys think you're taking me?" Daneka reminds her, "We said we're taking you away for the night." "Oh, no, I've got too much to do, I can't leave!" she cries. "Yes, you can, and you will!" I demand. "Yeah, you're not getting out of this one, Janny, we already had Raymond take care of everything," Tricie explains. "Does

Coleman know about this?" Janny asks. "Of course," Daneka answers, "do you honestly think we'd leave any stones unturned?" Janice takes a deep breath, reluctantly giving in, and looking back at Raymond. "Ray, is my book full tomorrow?" Raymond replies, "Janny, go get a life, or at least fake it for the next 24 hours!" We then grab her by the arms, escorting her out of the building. "You know you guys are nuts, right?" she exclaims. "Yeah, we know!" I admit. "Well, gimme my flowers and that Monet, and let's be teenagers!" Janny declares. We all laugh and head for the highway.

When we get to Washington, we go straight to the hotel. We have a four-bedroom suite that is set up like an apartment, but with a Jacuzzi. We had consumed the wine along the way, so we're acting very silly by the time we arrive. We all take showers and change clothes, and then take Janny out clubbing.

Our night is full of dancing, drinking, and flirting with just about anyone who will honor us. Janny says it's heaven to be with all of her friends like this, and she looks beautiful. She is wearing the black lace tee with the tight-fitting blue jeans and the cool black, block-heeled shoes I had bought for her. She even let us curl her hair and is wearing it down (we trashed the ponytail holder!).

Coleman would love to see this, but deep down, I'm glad that he won't. She looks too desirable.

We stay out until 1:30 in the morning. All of us are too drunk and silly to even have fun safely, so we decide to take it back to the hotel. Once we get back to the room, we pile up in the living room. Janny and I sit on the floor, and Janny lays her head in my lap as Daneka and Tricie lie down on the couch, just about passed out.

"I haven't had fun like this for far too long," says Janny. "Yeah, you need to get you ass out from behind that desk more often," I tell her. "You know, I don't know what I would do if I didn't have best friends like you guys," she says, using her foot to nudge Daneka and Tricie. They smile and we all have a group hug.

"Ooooh, wait! I'm going to see if the bellhop is in the hall. I want him to take a picture of us!" Tricie jumps up. Sure enough, he is at the end of the hallway. Tricie signals for him to come to the room. At this point, I'm hoping he'll only take a picture and not try to take anything else. We are all pretty drunk and probably wouldn't miss anything until the next morning.

He comes in and we all sit down on the couch. We are arm-in-arm and smiling our biggest smiles as he takes our picture. As he leaves, Tricie slips him five bucks for being so nice. We quickly return to our girl talk, catching up on the details we haven't had the chance to share during the course of our everyday lives. Tricie tells us how much she loves Andrew. Daneka talks about how she's looking forward to South Africa. I tell them about Joseph's promotion and how I might add on to our house. Janny mostly just listens.

Then Janny sits up and wraps her arm around my neck as she announces, "Well, ladies, I think I need a little something that you girls aren't able to provide for me." "You go, girl!" Tricie and Daneka give each other high fives. "What's that?" I ask, smiling. Janny leans over to whisper in my ear, "I'm in need of a stiff one, the kind only my husband can give me." The jealous lover in me begins to take over as I ask, "What are you going to do, have Coleman drive all the way here?" "He's already here. He called me this morning and said that he'd be working right outside Alexandria, so, if you'll excuse me..." She then gets up and stumbles over to the phone.

It takes every bit of strength I have to keep myself from pulling her away from it. Janny pages Coleman and he calls right back. I listen to her telling him where to come and how much she wants to be with him. By the time she hangs up the phone, I am so angry I can barely look at her. Meanwhile, Tricie and Daneka are on the floor, giggling about some joke Tricie is trying her best to remember.

"Is he coming?" I ask. "Yeah, I'm going to take a quick shower," she answers. "You know," I say standing and placing my hands on my hips, "this was supposed to be girls only!" I don't even feel the effects of the alcohol anymore. "Chill out!" Daneka threatens, "When you gotta have it, you gotta have it!" She and Tricie burst out laughing. "I think you two need to just sleep it off," I tell Daneka and Tricie. Tricie is already lying down with a pillow. "Taylor," Janny reasons, "this is supposed to be my birthday celebration. What better way to end it than in bed with my hubby?" She heads off to the bathroom to take a shower.

I sit and wait an hour and forty-five minutes for him to arrive. Tricie has long since gone back to her room, and Daneka is passed out on the couch. When I get up to check on Janny, I find her passed out on her bed. I stand in her doorway, looking at my best friend and thinking, I have some nerve being angry at her for wanting to see her own husband. But until we both come clean to our spouses, I have to share him, and Janny still has the upper hand.

My thoughts are interrupted by a knock at the door. I hurry to answer it, hoping that it won't wake anyone. Coleman is standing there, wearing a pair of sweat pants and a tee shirt. He's holding a gym bag in his hand. I look at him furiously and say in a quiet voice, "C'mon in, your lovely wife awaits you." "What did you think I was going to do, Taylor? She's my wife," Coleman says. "How is it that she knew exactly where to find you, yet I didn't, huh? Just answer that, Coleman!" I demanded in a whisper. "I left after you did, Taylor. I called the house, but when Joe answered the phone I knew you were already gone. Calm down," he urges. "I don't want you to be with her here, like this," I admit. "Have I ever questioned you about making love to Joe? The thought of it fucking eats me up inside, so I don't ask," he pleads. I begin to cry and he pulls me close to him. "Besides, I know when you do, it's me you're thinking about," Coleman reassures. "I can't handle the idea of you being with her anymore," I cry. "What did you expect me to do, Taylor, tell her I couldn't come and be with her because I'm in love with her best friend?" he asks, pointing at Janny's door. At that moment, Janny opens the door and comes into the front room. She finds Coleman holding my arms. "Coleman?" she asks, rubbing her eyes.

My back is to her, and in that moment I ponder whether I should just tell her right now and finally take control of something. But I remember what this night is all about and I back down. I stare into Coleman's eyes. He is unable to look back at me since his face is in clear view of Janice. "Look what the cat dragged in," I try to joke. Coleman looks at me for a moment with a half-hearted smile on his face. I see that this is killing him just as much as it is killing me. He goes to Janny and hugs and kisses her. "And you thought it couldn't get any better than this," I say, my voice beginning to crack. She takes Coleman by the hand and leads him back to her room, leaving me standing there alone. Coleman doesn't look back.

When the door closes behind them, I finally break down and begin to cry hard, walking to my room as fast as I can. I close the door and sob uncontrollably, trying my best to keep quiet. My door opens and Janny walks over to me. I keep my back turned to hide my tears. "Taylor . . . Taylor, I know you're upset, so turn around," she says. I face her and take her hand. "Are you okay, Taylor?" Janny is surprised to see just how upset I really am. "Don't do it, Janny," I say. "Don't do what, Taylor?" she asks, confused. I hesitate, angry at myself for allowing her to see me this upset. "Don't go and get yourself pregnant again," I say, making a quick save. "Believe me, girl, never again!" she reassures me. "But are you really okay about Coleman coming?" "Of course I am, enjoy it. I wish Joe was here right about now," I confess. Janny kisses me on the cheek and returns to her room.

It's the longest night of my life. I spend the majority of it imagining her making love to the man I want to spend the rest of my life with. My emotions bounce back and forth between anger and self-pity.

Tricie, Daneka and I awaken around noon the next morning and find Janny fast asleep in her bed, alone. We take her out for a late breakfast, take many more pictures together, and then begin our drive back home. On the way, we exchange our different versions of the night before.

Janny doesn't bring up how it was with Coleman, which doesn't surprise me. She is a private person who never shares much about her sex life. The only reason she said as much as she did last night was because she was exceedingly drunk. I imagine that her sex life is very straight-laced, because that would suit her personality.

When we reach Richmond, we all go our separate ways to carry out our Saturday activities. Janny is headed to her office, no doubt. Daneka goes to the gym to work out with her personal trainer, and Tricie heads to a poverty-stricken area of the city to teach a free class to four year olds. Joe, the kids and I spend our Saturdays together as a family. Our weekdays are so structured that when the weekends come, we usually just live them by the seat of our pants.

When I drive up to my house, I see my brother's rental car in the driveway. As I get out of the car, I can hear everyone in the back yard and smell charcoal burning. A cookout. I walk around the side of the house and through the wooden gate to find Joe Jr.

stumbling about the yard and Dawn and Bailey on the swings having an in-depth conversation – about Barbies, I'm sure. At the back of the yard, I see Joseph and my brother standing by the grill, talking and cooking. Both of them are holding beers in their hands.

The creaking fence catches the children's attention first. The three of them come running toward me, hugging me around my legs and nearly knocking me to the ground. The children's commotion causes both Adam and Joseph to look in my direction. My brother quickly comes over to hug and kiss me, and Joseph is right behind him. "Whassup, darlin'? How did it go?" Adam asks as I turn to Joseph, who kisses me on the lips. "What are you grilling, love?" I ask. "Shrimp! And some of that other famous cookout stuff for everyone else. Did Janny go home already?" Joe asks. "She's probably at her office. Coleman came to see her at the hotel. Anyway... can you put my bags upstairs, love?"

Joseph goes to the car to get my bags from the trunk. "Adam, how was your flight?" I ask. "It was okay. I had some punk tell me that there was a mistake with my ticket. My ticket wasn't showing that I was supposed to be in first class. Let's just say that by the time I finished with him, I had three upgrades out of the deal!" Adam brags. "It's always something," I commiserate, reaching down to pick up Joe Jr., who has now been tripped at least four times by his thoughtless sisters. In this house, only the strong survive!

Joseph comes out of the house through the back door and whispers in my ear, "I hope you don't have plans for tonight. I got something for you." "Oh, yeah? And what exactly might that be?" I pry. "Well, you're just going to have to wait and see." Joseph bites me on my earlobe, smiles and goes back to the grill to check on the food.

"I can't believe how big this boy is," Adam comments about Joe Jr.. I walk into the house carrying Joe Jr. through the back door and into the kitchen. "Have you been by to see Mommy and Daddy yet?" I ask. "No. I talked to them, though. They're coming over," Adam replies. "Did you talk to Lawrence?" I ask. "Yes. I'm thinking about bringing him out to New York with me." "Are you kidding me?" I retort. "He'll be in the mix so quickly your head will spin. Lawrence needs 24-hour attention. You know, Mom asked me a couple of times if I would let Lawrence stay here with Joe and me for a while, but I can't do it. I'm too busy trying to keep my family together."

"Don't sweat it, Taylor. Let's just try and enjoy the day, okay?" Adam suggests, placing his hand on my shoulder. Bailey brings Dawn into the house. "Mommy, may we have a drink, please?" "Of course, sweetie." Bailey opens the refrigerator and gets out a bottle of cranberry juice. She pours juice into two small cups for Joe Jr. and Dawn, and into a regular-sized plastic cup for herself.

"So, when is the last time you talked to Deandra?" Adam asks. "I haven't talked to her in about a week, but she sounded great," I reply. "Are they still trying to buy that house?" Adam asks. My sister and her husband, Grant, had been trying to buy a home for the past three months. Sadly, this life milestone that's supposed to be a wonderful experience for a couple was slowly turning into a nightmare for Deandra and Grant. Adam doesn't understand why it's such a big deal.

My brother has an unrealistic view about how marriage works. He has a throw-it-away-if-something-goes-wrong attitude about things, and doesn't understand why this concept doesn't work for relationships. I'm sure much of his attitude is the result of not really having a good parental example to go by. And he doesn't get to spend very much time with his married siblings, so he hasn't witnessed the the ups and downs of marriage that call for some give-and-take. He also hasn't had any serious relationships that require him to deal with challenges and commitment, until now.

"Is Tammy coming up today?" I ask while straightening up the kitchen. "No, she's working today. But you know what, Taylor? I can picture myself marrying her," Adam announces, shoving a strawberry in his mouth. "Really? And just what have you done with this picture?" I ask knowing that this revelation from Adam is going nowhere. Adam travels a lot and likes the idea of living out of a suitcase. He has told me on a couple of occasions that he would love to find a woman who would travel with him. I don't know Tammy, so I have no idea what her thoughts are on travel. He's a loving brother and a good uncle to his nieces and nephews, but he loves from a distance that prevents any of us from needing too much from him. A marriage is up close and personal, and with you all day, every day. He still, even at the age of 32, doesn't get it, and that's why I'm not in favor of my brother getting married.

"Tammy's kind of shy, Taylor," Adam continues. "Your friends would scare the crap out of her!" I smile and slap him on the arm, "What are you talking about, Adam?" "Well, look at them. I mean, Janny, she just took her size seven stilettos and kicked out the glass ceiling with them. Tricie has pretty much let blondes know that black girls can do it, too. And Daneka... Farrakhan, beware!" he exclaims.

"Oh, you'd be a wonderful advocate for the local feminist group. But my friends aren't like that, and you know it," I say defensively. "Actually," I add, "Daneka is just the kind of woman you need." "Don't get me wrong, Daneka is a beautiful woman all around," Adam says. "She's smart, attractive, all the things that I want in a woman. But I like to have the upper hand in my relationships."

I look out the window to check on things, and Joseph, who is about done with the grilling, motions for me to come to the back door. When I get there, he asks me to bring out the punch from the refrigerator. The food is ready, and now we can all sit down and catch up on what has happened to each of us over the past year.

I have loved my brother dearly since we were young. He often volunteered to play with me and was always there to protect me. He finally gave up the job of being my guardian about a year after Joe and I married.

My parents arrive late that evening. Not surprisingly, they have already eaten dinner, but didn't find it necessary to call and tell us that they wouldn't be eating with us. 'No problem,' I think to myself, 'we'll just donate those stacks of hamburgers and hot dogs to the nearest homeless shelter with a note attached saying "these weren't good enough for my parents to eat. Enjoy!"'

In spite of my annoyance, we actually delight in their company this time. We all enjoy listening to Dad tell stories about his childhood. My brother needs this visit more than we do. We can see my parents whenever we want, but he can only see them when he's in this part of the country.

The kids go to bed early. All the running around and climbing up and down from every adult's lap has worn them out. After Adam goes to bed, Joe and I take some wine up to our bedroom to drink while we gossip about our friends and just enjoy being together. We haven't been able to do this very often since Joe got his promotion.

We sit on the floor together, sipping wine. Joe tells me he's worried about me taking on so much during the day. He thinks I may be doing too much for everyone else and not focusing on our family. He's clearly trying to find out what has been pulling me farther and farther away from him this past year and a half. The truth is, I'm spending a lot of time inside my own mind, wrapped in my own thoughts. I'm always planning how to look, what to say and how to feel. The relationship with Coleman is taking a toll on my life at home. I'm a fool to think that I can carry on like this for much longer.

Suddenly, Joe stands up and says, "I want you to close your eyes." As I raise my hands to cover my eyes, I see him walk across the room and search through the bookcase. When he sits back down beside me, he places something in my lap. "Open your eyes," he says. I take my hands away from my face and look in my lap to find a brochure. More specifically, it's a brochure about Jamaica. "Do you mind elaborating?" I ask holding the brochure up and smiling. "How does the end of the month sound to you?" he asks. I put the brochure down on the floor, get up on my knees, and wrap my arms around his neck. "Is this just another way to get into my panties?" I joke. "I don't ever remember hearing you complain," Joe says.

He takes my glass out of my hand, places it on the floor and raises my arms above my head to remove my shirt. He closes the door and then walks back to stand in front of me, pulling his shirt over his head while I sit on the floor looking up at him. He reaches out for my hand and says, "Can we make love without inviting anyone else in tonight?" "What is that supposed to mean?" I ask, tilting my head. Joe sits down beside me with his legs stretched out in front of him and begins to kiss my neck, then down across my shoulder, biting my bra strap and pulling it down with his teeth. After he opens the front of my bra and strokes my bare breast with his hand, he grasps the back of my neck, pulls my face close to his and whispers in my ear, "Make love to me with *me* on your mind." Surprised, I pull away from him and look deep into his eyes, wondering if he means what I think he does by that statement, but he doesn't maintain eye contact for very long. Instead, he begins to kiss me as he pushes me back and pulls my shorts from under me, almost tearing them, all the while never letting his lips leave me. Joe is aggressive during lovemaking, which is one of the things I enjoy about him.

Feeling guilty, I decide to give it all I have, for Joe's sake. Breaking the kiss, I straddle his lap on my knees, running the flat of my hand across his bald head and down across his bare chest, licking different sections as I go. Joseph's body looks like it has been perfectly sculpted from rich, dark clay. He leans his head back and bites his bottom lip. As he does, I bend over him to suck on his right ear. He slides his hands underneath my panties and gets a tight grip on my rear end. I let go of his ear and decide to taste his mouth. Joe clenches fistfuls of my hair to keep me in place as we thrust our tongues deeply into each other.

I pull myself away from his mouth and teasingly kiss my way down toward his jeans. I stick my tongue deep into his navel as I open up the front of his jeans. He lifts his lower body up to help me pull his pants down, and I continue kissing as I go lower, finally taking a mouthful of his hard-on and sucking it vigorously as I massage his balls with my other hand. I glide my mouth up and down repeatedly, taking in every inch of him and watching his body jerk. Then I pull my mouth away and sit on his dick.

Joe sits up and grabs me by my waist to raise me up and down at the pace he wants. As we achieve a steady rhythm, Joe grits his teeth and pulls my body toward him, thrusting his penis deep inside me. Digging my nails into his shoulders, I arch my body to meet his every blow. I climax first, and as he watches me enjoy my orgasm, Joe comes right after me. Both of us are shiny with sweat. Breathing heavily, we conclude with a kiss, just as we began

8 OUTED

The weekend with my brother is a much-needed visit. I miss Adam and hate the fact that he has to travel so much. He leaves very early Monday morning, after I get up to eat breakfast with him. We talk about Mom and Dad, Tammy, and having children. Adam confides that he's hoping to get a new position that will keep him closer to home and give him the opportunity to put more time into his social and love lives. After breakfast he calls a cab, kisses me goodbye and heads for the airport.

After my brother leaves, I go back to bed, hoping that my children will have mercy on their mother's exhausted soul and sleep late. A little before 7:30, I am awakened by a knock at the front door. Not realizing the time, I wait for Joseph to answer it.

When the knocking continues, I jump out of bed, grab my robe and hurry down the steps to see who it is. "Who's there?" I ask, looking through the peephole. My eyes haven't adjusted yet. "It's me, Taylor, open up." I realize that it's Daneka and open the door.

Daneka walks in briskly and sets her purse down on the coffee table. "What are you doing here so early?" I ask, sitting down on the couch. "Is Joe still here?" she asks walking down the hallway to look into the kitchen. "No, he's gone, you want some coffee?" I yawn. "No, Taylor, I don't want any coffee. I don't know how to beat around the bush, so I'm just going to tell you..." "What's wrong?" I ask.

"I was awake when Coleman came to the hotel Friday night," Daneka admits, "and I heard you guys arguing." My mouth drops open in shock, but I'm silent, not denying anything. Daneka looks me up and down, then shakes her head, saying, "Taylor, please tell me that you're not having an affair with Coleman." In shame, I cover my face with my hands and begin to cry, quietly saying, "I can't do that." Daneka gets very angry and repeats, "Goddammit, Taylor, tell me that you are not having an affair with Coleman, your best friend's husband!" I can't look up and continue to cry behind my hands. Daneka squats down and yanks my hands away from my face, forcing me to look at her. "I can't tell you that it's not true, Daneka, because it is... Coleman and I have a relationship."

Daneka sucks her teeth in a huff, stands up and walks away from me. "A relationship? A *relationship*, Taylor?! Just tell me this, how does a married woman have a *relationship* with a married man? Unless it's a friendship... and that's not what we're talking about here." She looks at me with fiery eyes.

Breaking the silence between us, I finally say, "Daneka, I have been attracted to Coleman ever since the first time I met him." "Then why did you marry Joseph?" she demands. "I don't know," I answer miserably. "This is fucking ridiculous!" Daneka grabs her purse and walks toward the door to leave. I jump up and grab her arm to stop her. Aggravated, she pulls away. I plead, "Can you imagine having what you think is a fairy tale life, with three beautiful children, a home, financial stability, and a husband that loves you completely, and realizing five years in that you've always been in love with another man? And even worse, that the man is married to your best friend? My life has become pure hell, all because of love," I say as I wipe at the tears on my face.

Daneka smiles disgustedly. "You're pathetic. I would never have expected this from you, Taylor. You talk about how your fairy tale lifestyle has become hell, but you *chose* to do this! You think I'm going to have pity on you for something that you knowingly did even though it was wrong? How do you think Joseph would feel if he knew? What about your children, Taylor? Shit! What about Janny and Jolie? Why drag them down to hell with you?" Daneka begins to cry. "Shame on you. Shame on your selfish little stupid ass." She storms through the foyer and slams the front door behind her.

I sit down on the couch and break down. Portions of our argument are flying around in my mind, and it feels as if the room is spinning. Over and over I see the faces of Joe, Janny, Coleman, Tricie, Bailey, Dawn, Joe Jr., and Jolie. I keep thinking about what I've done and how it will affect everyone around me. The only thing that feels right is the love in my heart for Coleman. Why does love cause so much pain?

"Mommy... Mommy." I awaken to find Dawn pulling on my arm. I had cried myself to sleep on the couch. "I'm hungry," Dawn pleads. I pull her in and lay her down beside me, stroking her hair and realizing how much she looks like her father. "I'm sorry, Dawn, Mommy fell asleep. Are your sister and brother awake, too?" I ask her. "Yes, they're upstairs in Joe Jr.'s room."

I start my day almost like any other day. As I head for the kitchen to make French toast and sausage for breakfast, Dawn follows me and sits on a stool at the counter to be near me. 'What if I leave Joseph for Coleman?' I think. 'Will Joe take my children away from me?' Unable to handle the idea of being without them, I shut this line of thought down by focusing on the children and our morning routine.

When breakfast is over, we all get dressed and spend most of the day in the yard. I can't stop thinking about my altercation with Daneka, and it makes me feel sick. I'm not too concerned about her telling Janny or Joseph – that would be letting me off too easy.

Joseph comes home for lunch and can tell that I'm not myself. He asks if I'm okay and I tell him I'm not feeling well. He says he'll call Kim from work to see if she can babysit tonight, but I tell him that I'll just take a nap when the kids do. I don't want to be alone; I need to be surrounded by my family today.

While the kids and I are eating dinner, I realize I should let Coleman know what happened this morning with Daneka. Bailey and Dawn are done eating, so they quickly clear their plates and head off to the computer, but Joe Jr. isn't done yet. While the girls are busy downstairs and Joe Jr. clearly has another 20 minutes or so to go, I call Coleman. To my surprise, Janny answers the phone. I look at the clock to check the time. It's only 6:00; Janny is never home this early. "Hey, girl, what are you doing home?" I ask. "Jolie's piano recital is tonight. What's going on?" she asks. "Nothing... I called your office and they told me that you left early," I lie. "Yeah, you know, I'm never home this time of day. Where are the kids?" she asks. "Bailey and Dawn are downstairs and Joe Jr. is right here, still eating. What time are you guys leaving?" I ask. "Ten minutes ago! I'll call you when I get back." "All right, Janny. Kiss Jolie for me," I say. "Later, girl." We hang up.

As soon as I put the phone back on the receiver, it rings again. Startled, I pick it up saying, "Hello." "Taylor, it's me," Daneka says. I want so badly to talk to her. I need her to be a friend and listen. I'm not angry at her for telling me off this morning; I'm just hoping she'll give me an opportunity to explain the whole situation. "Daneka, I hope you'll let me tell you what's going on," I say. "That's why I called," she admits. I sit down in the chair next to Joe Jr., who is now making smiley faces with his peas, and try to explain. "We've been seeing each other since the end of last March. I've had feelings for Coleman ever since Joe and I started dating back in college, but I didn't succumb to my feelings back then because staying with Joe made more sense. Coleman was so immature and unstable. Even after he married Janny, I had a place in my heart for him. But it wasn't until last year that I realized I truly love him. The problem is that I love Joseph, too. Not only is Joseph the man I married; he is the man I needed at that time. The horrible irony is that his love for me has given me the courage to admit to myself who I really love."

Daneka finally speaks; "Taylor, I could always count on you to make good decisions. I relied on you for that. Doing this is

360 degrees from the norm." "Well, you've expected too much from me. Who decided that I should always be the one to set the standard?" I ask. I know that what I'm doing is wrong, but it seems so unfair that the one thing I finally am sure that I want is almost unattainable. "Taylor, there's just nothing right about this affair. You're risking your married life to have something that feels good at the moment..." Daneka says. "Daneka," I interrupt, "I'm risking my married life to finally do something I need for myself. I can't imagine myself 20 years from now being exactly like my mother. I know you don't understand. I'm sorry I have taken away some of the trust you have in our relationship, but I love Coleman and no matter how things turn out, that's a fact that will never change." "Taylor, you're a fool if you think Coleman will ever leave Janny and Jolie for you," she says. I don't speak, so Daneka continues, "And I hate you for putting me in this position. I love Janny, and my first instinct as a friend is to tell her that her husband's cheating on her, but how do I tell her that the woman he's involved with is our friend? I'm turning my back on this – it's too much, Taylor. I won't be your sounding board and I won't give you advice, but I will tell you this: if you and Coleman really do love each other like

you say, 'fess up and tell your spouses." "I gotta go, Daneka, Joe is home." We hang up.

Joseph drops his briefcase in a chair and picks up the mail from the desk, looking through it as he starts down the hallway to the kitchen. I meet him halfway and greet him with a hug and a kiss. I know that my days with Joe are numbered. I love him so dearly, love everything about him, but I realize that we just aren't meant to spend the rest of our lives together. I can explain that to Daneka and Coleman. Hell, I've even figured out how to explain it to Joseph and my sweet children. But how do I explain it to my heart?

The next morning I call Coleman to tell him that Daneka overheard us that night in the hotel. Coleman is most concerned about her feelings toward me, and about whether or not she is going to take it upon herself to tell Janny. He wants her to know that he does love me and plans to make a situation that started out wrong, end right. "I have to go downtown anyway, so I'm going to stop by her office," Coleman tells me just before he hangs up.

Coleman sits in the waiting area on the 27th floor, waiting to see Daneka. Deep in thought, he vaguely hears footsteps come down the hallway and stop at the receptionist's desk. As the steps

come closer, Coleman realizes they are Daneka's. She greets him

with a hug. "I'll bet I know why you're here," she smiles. "Let's

go to my office." Daneka leads Coleman through La Negra, Inc.,

where noisy teams of writers are rushing around the bullpen. When

they reach her office, she closes the door behind them. "Have a

seat," she insists, as she sits down at the other end of her couch.

Daneka removes her glasses and places them in her lap. Coleman

looks at the walls of Daneka's office, which are covered with

award plaques and framed articles. He breaks the silence; "Are all

of these yours?" "Uh huh, the ones I'm proudest of," Daneka

answers.

"I don't know what Taylor told you... and I don't want to

know because I don't want this to look like any kind of collusion. I

don't know where to begin really... " Coleman leans forward, folds

his hands together and continues; "Janny is a high-maintenance

woman who prefers a high-maintenance lifestyle. For a long time

she wanted a high-maintenance man, and that's never been me. I

don't know how much you talk about us when you get together,

but Janny only loves one thing in her life, and I don't need to tell you that it's her job. When we first got married, I thought that having Jolie would change that, but now I'm sorry that I pressured her into having a child. In hindsight, I realize that I was trying to turn Janny into Taylor. Now, I want to be with a woman who is in love with me. I want to spend the rest of my life with the woman I've always loved, and that's Taylor."

"I just don't understand why you married Janny if you never loved her," Daneka says. "In a way, I wanted to get back at Taylor for marrying Joseph," Coleman says truthfully. "And I thought that over time I would forget about Taylor. But I didn't realize how much I loved her." "Do you think it's worth risking everything for?" Daneka probes. "I can't answer that. I do know that Taylor means more to me than Janny, and that I've been anxious for her to tell Joseph so that we can be together openly. But I can't stand the thought of her leaving her family only because I pressured her, because then I'll be in the same situation I'm in right now with Janice. And I don't know if she has really considered the thought of being without her children. If I would always have to worry about her leaving me to get her children back, I don't know if I could go through with this. Regardless, I plan to tell Janny something soon. I can't keep on like this..."

Daneka's speakerphone interrupts them; "Ms. Smith, you have a call on line three, would you like to take it?" Daneka walks over to the phone and picks up the receiver. "Who is it?" Daneka asks, then, "tell her I'll be with her in a minute." She turns to Coleman, "I've got to take this call. It's Sharon, and I told her I'd meet her for lunch."

"Yeah, I gotta go, too," Coleman says. He stands and walks toward the door. "Coleman, take care of this, okay?" Daneka reminds him. Coleman walks out without a word, closing the door behind him.

The next morning I'm in the basement cleaning out the storage area, which over the years has become the junk area. Joseph is in the front yard with the kids. He had promised Bailey that she could plant some roses. I hear Joseph calling my name, "Taylor! Taylor!" "Yeah," I yell. "Janny's here." I run upstairs and out the front door, just in time to see Janny closing the gate and walking up the sidewalk.

"Hi, Joseph. I wish I could get Coleman to do that with Jolie, but I guess that's what we pay the gardener for, huh?" she says. She comes up to me and greets me with a hug saying, "What are you working on?" "The storage room," I answer as we walk inside and head for the kitchen, "I'm tired of looking at it. You want some water?" "Yes, I'll take a glass. So, I'm inviting you guys to my house next Thursday. I'm having a dinner party, and I might even cook this time!" she says, sipping her water. I look at Janny, tilt my head and open my eyes wide in amazement. "Okay, maybe that's pushing it," she says, "but I have made time to entertain, so you should be proud of me." I bend over jokingly, and say, "I'm not worthy." She turns and walks toward the door, grabbing an apple just before leaving. "Seven-thirty... and bring the kids. I'm even providing childcare!" she looks back at me smiling, waves goodbye and walks through the door.

Later that night, Joseph and I gather with the kids in the den for one more viewing of Pinocchio. Joseph is at his desk working on contracts. Bailey and Dawn are sitting beside me on the couch, and Joe Jr. is playing on the floor beside his father's feet. "Did Janny tell you about next Thursday?" I ask. "No, what's going on

129

next Thursday?" he asks. "Janny is hosting a dinner party." "With

or without pay?" Joe asks jokingly. "Ha! Ha! Ha!" I say

sarcastically. "It's at 7:30; will you be home?" "Yeah, I'll be here.

What's the occasion?" he asks. "I don't know. She just said she's

entertaining." I end the conversation by going into the kitchen to

grab a banana.

I really have no idea why Janny is having this party. The

last time she had a dinner party, it was to celebrate her promotion

at Chinson, but I knew about that a week before the event. This

time I have no clue about what Janny has up her sleeve.

The next afternoon, I'm getting the kids' backpacks together

for camp when the phone rings. I glance at my watch and realize

I'm already 10 minutes late, so I decide not to answer it. But my

baby girl has a different idea. Dawn picks up the receiver; "Hello?

Hi, Tricie... I'm fine. You wanna talk to my Mommy? Okay...

MOM, TRICIE'S ON THE PHONE!" she yells. I smile at Dawn

and say, "Thank you, sweetie pie, Hello? Hi, Tricie. Yeah, I was

on my way out the door, why? What's up? What time? Okay, I'll

be there." I hang up and rush my kids out the door.

Just as I reach the porch and turn to lock the door, I notice Coleman driving up in front of the house. He has a very serious look on his face. He parks, jumps out of the car and meets me halfway up the sidewalk. "Hi, Mr. Colebury," Bailey greets. "How are you, Bailey?" he asks, smiling and opening the gate for us. "Is everything okay?" I ask. "Yeah, I just wanted to talk to you about something," he says as he helps me get the kids into the car. After I close Bailey's door, I say, "Not in front of the kids, Coleman, you know that." "I know, Taylor. Can you meet me at Teariffic after you drop them off?" he asks. "Of course, but I won't have much time, I'm meeting Tricie, Daneka and Janny for lunch." Coleman turns to walk to his car. I call out to him and he turns around. I mouth to him silently, "I love you." He smiles.

After dropping off Bailey, Dawn, and Joe Jr., I drive downtown to Teariffic. As I enter, I see Coleman sitting in the waiting area. I notice that he's wearing an olive green dress shirt with a pair of black pants. He stands as I approach him and kisses me on my mouth. "You look nice," I tell him. The hostess seats us near the back and I begin the conversation. "So, what exactly are you guys celebrating?" I ask. "I don't know for sure, but I know she's been making a lot of calls to Washington State, and this morning, I got a call from a Mount Prior Boarding School in Washington State telling me that it isn't too late to register Jolie for this fall," Coleman says. "So, you think she..." Coleman interrupts, "I'm not positive, but if you think back, the last time Janice took a night off to entertain was when she was promoted to President at Chinson." Coleman leans across the table and holds my hands tightly continuing, "I won't stay in my marriage, Taylor, and I'm not going to Washington. I'm asking you to be with me." I stare into his eyes and am silent.

"Do you realize you might lose the kids, Taylor?" he asks. "Yes, Coleman, I think about that almost every waking moment of the day, but I can't go on like this." I begin to cry, Coleman lifts my chin and kisses me. Our caress is interrupted by a familiar voice. "Hi, Mr. and Mrs. Colebury." When I pull away from Coleman, I look up to find Kim standing before us. "Mrs. Wayland... I didn't know... I'm sorry... I thought you were Mrs. Colebury... how are you, Mr. Colebury?" she stammers. "I'm doing alright," Coleman answers. "I'm going to have a regular tea with milk, Kim," I order. "Nothing for me," Coleman decides. Kim hurries away. At that moment, I decide not to do this anymore. It isn't fair to anyone. "Let me just have this last celebration with Janny, and I'll tell Joseph Thursday night." Coleman agrees and we set the date. Now I am off to have lunch with my dear friends, for what will probably be one of the last meetings we all have as friends.

9 PAIN AND MORE PAIN

We are supposed to be meeting at Walby's Diner at noon,
but I arrive early so I decide to get a booth and wait for everyone
else to arrive. To my surprise, Janny gets there just a few minutes
later. Janny isn't usually early for anything, except her meetings at
work. "Hey, girl, what are you doing here so early?" Janny asks. "I
was down here after I dropped the kids off at Camp, so I thought
I'd just come in and wait," I answer. "Coleman's down here, too,"
she comments. "He promised to pick up paint for the Florida room.
I want the painters to get in there before tomorrow so that come
Thursday, my guests won't be overcome by paint fumes." Just as
Janny finishes that sentence, Beatrice comes bouncing around the
corner, "What's up, guys? I can't believe you're both here early.
Where's Daneka?" she asks. "I don't know. I've only been here for

10 minutes, and Janny just got here. So, what's going on?" I ask.

Janny taps my arm, "Hold your horses; wait 'til Daneka gets here."

Tricie promises, "It'll be worth the wait. God knows it's been

murder for me."

"I'm here, I'm here, and will you look at this, a full house!"

says Daneka as she approaches the booth and slides in next to

Tricie. "I had to stop off and pay my cable bill," Daneka explains.

"Now there's a woman who's got her priorities straight," Janny

comments, and we all laugh.

"Okay," Tricie says, "I asked you guys to come here today

because I have something to tell you and I hope you will be as

happy as I am, so here goes... Andrew asked me to marry him, and

I said yes!" We all jump up to hug and congratulate Tricie. The

commotion causes many of the other patrons to look over, and a

server motions for us to be quiet.

"When did he ask, Tricie?" I ask. "Yesterday morning. We

had gotten our parents together at his grandmother's cottage for the

weekend, and his mother called us downstairs for breakfast. When

we got down there, his mother and father had really serious looks

on their faces. When we sat down at the table, Andrew's father stood up to say grace. He said, "You know I don't approve of you two dating anymore," and Andrew said, "You know, Dad, you're right." He walked around the table to me, got down on one knee and said, "Mr. and Mrs. Arthur, Mom, Dad, I stand before all of you today to promise to dedicate the rest of my life to this woman, who sheds a more meaningful light on each day, who has taught me the real meaning of devotion, and whose every touch still sends chills up my spine. Beatrice Marie Arthur, will you be my beautiful bride?" I thought I would pass out! I couldn't believe everyone knew all weekend why we were there except me!"

"Tricie, that's beautiful. I think you guys will be good for each other," Daneka says, smiling. "Everyone loves a wedding, so when's the day?" Janny asks. "Well, that leads me to my question," says Tricie. "Taylor, can we get married at your house?" I look at Tricie and feel everyone's eyes on me. "Before you answer, I just want to tell you why I would like to be married at your house. We were on our first real date when we came to your house, and that's where you all got to meet him for the first time. Your place is sentimental for us," Tricie finished.

"I could never say no to you, Tricie, I'd be honored to have your wedding in my home." I lean over and kiss Tricie on the cheek. "Well, the reception is on me!" exclaims Janny. "Oh good, that was going to be my next question. The date will be September 16th, so Daneka, you're going to have to find yourself a man, since it won't be two and two anymore!" Daneka smiles. "On that note, I'd like to make a toast to Tricie and Andrew – I wish you a lifetime of love together!" We raise our water glasses. After the toast, Daneka avoids eye contact with me.

Thursday morning comes sooner than I expect. I don't even remember what I did the day before. When I feel Joseph climbing out of bed, I pull him back. Joe leans over me. "I gotta go," he whispers. "Stay a little while," I beg, kissing him. Joe lies on top of me to kiss me back, and we make love. I am going to tell my husband I am in love with his best friend tonight, but right now, I want to make love to him. I want to feel close to him this one last time. I also need to know if, after making love to Joe, I have any doubts about Coleman. Memories of our wedding day and the days our children were born flash through my mind. I have loved the times I've had with Joseph, but it's time to make a choice, one that will change my life forever.

At a quarter to seven that evening, I'm sitting on the edge of our bed in my underwear, combing Dawn's hair. Bailey and Joe Jr. are already dressed and playing in Bailey's room. Joseph is just coming in the door. As he comes up the steps, he yells out, "It's not my fault!" "Daddy, Daddy!" Bailey and Joe Jr. run to their father. Dawn jumps out of my arms just as I finish the braid in her hair, to join them. By the time he reaches the doorway of our bedroom, he has Joe Jr. on his shoulders, Bailey on his back, Dawn in his arms, and his briefcase in his teeth. He lets the briefcase fall and asks, "How was your day?" "Okay," I say. "I didn't think you were going to make it. Are you planning to change?" "Yeah, just let me grab a quick shower," he says, taking the kids back into Bailey's bedroom to play.

While he's in the shower, I put on my floor-length fuchsia dress with spaghetti straps, which is form fitting and backless. I add my strappy black shoes and fuchsia pearl drop earrings. After his shower, Joseph puts on his black suit with a white silk banded-collar shirt, and adds his black Coach belt. He is handsome, indeed. "You look beautiful, love," Joseph comments, hugging me around my waist. I look deeply into his eyes, feeling love and pain all at once. "Do you know how much you've changed my life for the better?" I say. "Why don't you tell me," he says, taking my hand and wrapping it around his neck. "I never knew love until I met you," I tell him as I kiss him gently on the lips. Then we herd the children out the door for the drive to the Colebury house.

Janny's "estate" sits on ten acres of land. Tara is a cottage compared to this place! At the border of the grounds stands a 15-foot fence, which is usually closed but is open tonight because of the number of people she has probably invited. The circular driveway leads to the front of the house, where a valet is waiting. We all get out and walk up the stairs to the double front doors, which are both open. Twin turrets flank the covered entry, and a huge half-moon window framed in stone overlooks the doorway.

"May I take your shawl, Ma'am?" a maid asks as I enter the foyer. "Please," I answer, handing her my wrap. Off to the left is a winding staircase that matches the marble floor in the entry.

Janny, looking great as usual, soon walks in to greet us. She has her hair pulled into a bun and wrapped in gold netting that matches her dress. With short blousy sleeves, a round neckline, and an A-line that flows to the floor, the dress and the woman in it are elegant and classy. "I'm so glad you guys are here," Janny says. Why don't you little ones go upstairs and play with Jolie while Mommy and Daddy come on in and join the grown-ups." As the kids scramble up the stairway, Janny leads us straight through the foyer, past the study on the right, and into the sunken gathering room where about 15 of her other guests, mostly people from her job, are already mingling.

The gathering room has a fireplace surrounded by stone that soars to the top of the two-level vaulted ceiling. Above the mantel is a painting of Jolie. The hearthstone matches the stone in the entrance and out on the terrace. French doors, all leading to the outdoors, encircle the front half of the room.

To the left of the gathering room is the Florida room. Janny has two benches in that room for anyone who might wish to sit and admire her carefully tended potted plants, although none of us ever do. Behind the Florida room is the kitchen, where her cooking staff are busy preparing dinner.

Janny's elegant formal dining room is adjacent to the foyer. Her great-grandmother's dining room table, which is large enough to seat 25 people, occupies center stage. The walls are covered with dark burgundy wallpaper with a beautiful hunter green stripe-and-paisley design. Janny loves her home and has put a lot of thought and effort into creating it. Unfortunately, she doesn't spend much time here.

While chatting with some of Janny's friends in the gathering room, I notice that Daneka has walked in. She sees me and comes over, and I greet her with a hug. "How long have you been here?" she asks. "About 15 minutes," I answer. "You look beautiful!" I tell her. Daneka has her hair down. She's wearing a long-sleeved, short black dress. The sleeves and neckline are sheer to just above her breasts, where the fabric becomes solid black. She's wearing sheer black pantyhose and black patent leather sandals. "Did you bring the kids?" Daneka asks. "Yes, they're upstairs with Jolie and her sitter," I answer. "Is Joe here?" Daneka asks. I point toward the study, "He's in there with Coleman." Daneka reaches out to hold my hand, "I love you, Taylor. You know that, right?" she asks. "I know," I answer, giving her another hug.

Soon, Tricie and Janny join us. Tricie is wearing a black silk pantsuit. The front of the jacket is outlined with small, gold buttons, and her gold shoes match the buttons perfectly. Her hair is pulled back from her face and hanging down her back. "Don't we look lovely, girls," Tricie says, smiling and wrapping her arms around our shoulders. "Oh, Janny!" she adds, "Andrew had to pick Trevor up from softball practice, so will you let me know when he gets here?" "Isn't that cute, they're doin' the baseball thing!" Janny teases. "But listen, girl, unless he gets here in the next five minutes, he'll miss dinner." Janny leaves them to greet other guests.

Just as Janny warned, dinner is announced just a few minutes later. We all gather in the dining room to bless the food. The menu includes broiled chicken, lobster patties, steamed trout, baked stuffed shrimp, scallops wrapped in bacon, fresh steamed vegetables, and hot rolls. Everything is delicious.

I don't see Coleman until dinner. I've been nervous for most of the night thinking about what I need to do. Tricie, who is next to me at the table, mutters, "I'm going to kill Andrew! Trevor hasn't eaten since lunch!" "Andrew probably stopped off at

McDonald's on the way. You know how responsible he is when it comes to the kids. When he realized how late it was, he probably stopped to get Trevor something to eat," I say trying to console her. "I know, you're probably right. I told him not to be late, though." Joe leans over me, "I'll make sure to tell him how good it was!" he smiles, and we continue to eat.

After dinner, Janny invites everyone into the gathering room for warm brandy and sherbet. Once everyone is served, she motions for Coleman to stand next to her and taps her glass. "Excuse me, everyone, if I could have your attention for a moment... I'd like to thank you all for coming to our home this evening. I can't think of anything I enjoy more than being surrounded by my closest friends and colleagues and sharing a good meal, but now I'd like to get to the matter at hand... Coleman," she smiles and reaches for his hand, continuing, "Chinson Chemical has offered me a position in Washington State." Everyone applauds. 'Coleman was right,' I think to myself. Janny continues, looking at Coleman, "And my darling, sweet husband, I think we're going to have to take this position for financial reasons if nothing else, so we can buy a bigger house...

preferably one with a nursery! I'm pregnant!" She embraces

Coleman. The look on his face is utter shock.

I grab my mouth, also in shock, suddenly feeling nauseous.

I use my other hand to clutch my stomach. Joe sees the look on my

face and asks, "you alright?" Daneka looks over at me from the

other end of the terrace and begins to make her way over to me.

Unable to speak, I rush to the powder room. I close the door, step

to the sink and splash cold water on my face. By now my feelings

of disbelief are turning into indignation.

Hearing the door open, I look up in the mirror to see

Coleman's reflection. He comes in and closes the door behind him.

"Taylor, I didn't know anything about the baby!" I ask, "What the

hell is going on, Coleman?" He explains, "Taylor, I had no idea

she would even try to get pregnant, let alone keep it. You know

how Janny feels about having any more kids." "Why didn't you

use anything, Coleman?" I ask. "I did, most of the time. I just

never thought... please," he reaches for my hand. I pull away and

begin to cry and become erratic, "This probably happened in

Washington, DC. She was too fucking wasted to remember to use

her diaphragm. I can't believe this is happening. I trusted you. I was going to leave Joseph tomorrow. How could you let this happen?" "Taylor, nothing has changed between us, this wasn't planned!" he insists. "Bullshit, Coleman, you just used me to fulfill your greatest fantasy, and I fell for it. Well, congratulations!" I try to open the door to leave while Coleman stops me, "Taylor, you can't just run out there like this. You gotta remember there are a lot of people out there. They'll know something's up with you acting like this. You know this baby isn't going to just make me stay with Janice. I'll still tell her about us tomorrow. Just calm down for a minute," he says. "Really? You mean to tell me that even though you know she's pregnant with your child, you're still going to leave?" I ask. "Taylor, I didn't ask for this." I argue, "Every time you had unprotected sex with her, you asked for it! I thought it was finally going to happen for us, Coleman."

I tug at the door again and Coleman pushes against it. With more force, I eventually snatch open the door. Janny, Daneka, Joseph and Tricie are standing in the hallway just outside the door. Daneka is restraining Janny by her shoulders. I can only see Joseph's profile. He has his head tilted back and both hands in his pockets, and is jingling his keys. He can't even stand to look at me. "Taylor?" Tricie asks innocently.

Shocked, I open my mouth to speak, but before I can say anything, Janny pulls away from Daneka, looks at me and then at Coleman, and says, "I'd ask if this was some kind of goddamned joke, but I don't remember either of you being bright enough to have a comedic side. Just tell me this, Taylor: when you tried to talk me out of having that abortion I had in Chicago, was it really because you were fucking my husband?" I stammer, "Janny, I... "

"DON'T... don't even try to explain a goddamned thing because I've heard enough. And you, Coleman..." she continues. "I've had so many proposals from much more eligible men than you, and I turned them down, only to be cheated on by a sorry-ass, blue collar sonofabitch like you!" She looks at Coleman. "Get the fuck out of my house and take this bitch with you!"

Janny strides to the door to show us out. When she opens the door, two police officers are standing there. One officer greets Janny with, "Good evening, Ma'am, we are sorry to disturb you, but is there a Beatrice Arthur here?" Janny wipes a tear from her face and answers, "Yes, there is . . . Tricie!"

Tricie comes to the door and looking at the officers, says, "Yes?" The officer continues, "Ms. Arthur?" "What is it?" she says. "Your neighbor told us we could find you here. Was your car stolen tonight?" "I don't think so. My fiancé has it... but he was supposed to be here over two and a half hours ago, so maybe that's what happened!" she answers. "Was he alone?" the officer asks. "No, he has my son with him." The two officers look at the each other, then back at Tricie. "Ms. Arthur, we need you to come down to the station with us." "Why?" Tricie asks. "I think you should come down to the station so that..." Tricie interrupts," Tell me what's going on!" "Ms. Arthur, your car was involved in a fatal accident."

Daneka grabs my hand and Janny wraps her arms around Tricie. Tricie studies the officer's face as to not miss anything he says. The officer continues, "The driver was identified as Andrew Mason, the passenger was an unidentified black male child... there were no survivors." Hearing his, Tricie collapses to her knees, grabs both of her ears and screams, "NO, NO, NO!" The sound of her shrill cries echoes in my head and my mind goes blank. I felt empty. This night wasn't supposed to be like this.

The four of us get into Janny's car and drive to the police station to identify the car. It is Tricie's car. Then we meet Andrew's parents at the hospital to identify Andrew and Trevor's bodies. The car was flattened by a tractor-trailer. The doctors tell Tricie that they both died instantly.

During the two car rides, no one speaks. The tension is thick enough to choke me, but I have to be there for Tricie. I didn't want Janny to find out like this. She's my best friend, and if I could change things, I wouldn't have had the affair with Coleman at all. But I had.

As we leave the hospital, Janny stops me in the parking lot and, in tears, asks me, "Why, Taylor? Why didn't you just do this back in '89, huh? We all knew you two were flirting back then, but why did you pursue it after I married him?" "I didn't want to love him, Janny," I answer. Furious, Janny yells, "IS THAT SUPPOSED TO MAKE ME FEEL BETTER?" Tricie sobs louder on Daneka's shoulder. Daneka looks over her shoulder at me and says, "Not now, and not here, guys. Taylor, just go home." Janny turns abruptly and walks to her car, and Daneka and Tricie follow slowly behind. I watch them drive away.

I take a cab home. As I stick the key in the door, I think briefly about not going in at all, but I know I must face Joseph. I have to show him the respect he deserves after what I've done to our family.

As I enter the house, I notice that all the lights are off. Before I can reach for the wall switch, a light comes on in the den. All I can see is the back of Joseph's head. He is sitting on the couch, and beside him on the table is a half empty bottle of gin. As I stand there in the foyer staring at the back of his head, I can smell the alcohol.

Joseph slowly reaches out his arm and lays his wedding band down on the table. Before turning to face me, he says, "You couldn't just be happy with me and our kids. You couldn't just be happy with four devoted friends..." I stay silent and listen. "No, when you wanted what you wanted, it didn't matter how anyone else might feel." Joe stands. He's still in his suit pants. His shirt is unbuttoned and his shoes and socks are by his feet. He looks sloppy – as if his body has taken a beating along with his heart.

He continues, pointing his finger at his chest, "I invested my heart, my time, my money, my soul, my motherfuckin' life in this marriage, only to have you shit all over it for an audience to witness! Taylor, what the hell were you thinking? What the hell could you have possibly said to convince yourself that it was okay to fuck my boy?" I look away.

"This ain't no soap opera; we won't break for a fuckin' commercial and then go back to our everyday lives... What was I supposed to do to make it right? What more could I have done for you to have enough love? Maybe I should have just built a damn white picket fence around the house! Would that have made it right? Would that have looked normal enough for you to be happy?" Joseph yells with rage. He grabs his wedding band and throws it through the open window saying, "Is that what's missing?" Startled, I raise my hands to my ears. Joseph races up to me and begins to kiss me wildly while yanking and tearing the straps on my dress. "You want me to fuck you harder? Is that it? Wasn't my dick big enough?"

"Stop, Joseph, stop!" I cry. I try to pull away when I hear Dawn at the top of the stairs, saying, "Daddy?" Still struggling with Joseph in his drunken state, I yell at him, "Joe, Dawn is at the top of the stairs!"

Grasping onto my waist, Joe drops to his knees and begins to cry. I hold him close to me, fighting back tears, and say, "Dawn, it's okay, sweetie, go back to bed." Joe buries his head against my stomach and says, "I've gone over it again and again in my head, Taylor, and I can't forgive you for what you've done. I believed in us, but I don't think you ever did." "Yes, I did, Joseph," I say earnestly. "Only for what you needed from it!" he snaps. You never loved me. You might have wanted to, but you never wanted to be my wife as much as I wanted you to be," he says. I bow my head shamefully as the truth hits me.

Joseph stands up, walks back to the couch and sits down. "Take the checkbook and the car. I'll pay for your hotel tonight, and tomorrow my lawyer will contact you. The kids will be staying here with me." I cry aloud as my worst fears are realized. Joseph shuts off the light and lays his head back. My instincts tell me to run upstairs and grab the kids and take them with me, but I realize I've done enough wrong. Dragging them with me to uncertainty would only make things worse.

I feel the need to explain. "I tried to make it right, Joseph. I tried to ignore my feelings but the lies became too much to handle.

151

I'm sorry." After taking another gulp of gin, he says, "You can come for your things after we leave tomorrow." I turn around and walk out the front door. As I close the door behind me, my knees buckle and I nearly fall to the ground. I can't believe what I've done to all the people I love the most. I feel as though my whole world is being crushed.

Trevor and Andrew's funeral services are held that Sunday afternoon. I attend, but purposely arrive late so as to not distract from the service. I was always the first person to hold Tricie when she cried, and I love her children like they are my own. I can't imagine the magnitude of her pain.

When I drive up to the cemetery, most of the procession is gone. I walk across the grounds toward the burial sites, which are still being covered by the groundsmen. As I get closer, I notice that someone is still sitting there. It's Tricie. She looks up at me and we embrace, cry and wipe each other's tears.

"I'm so sorry, Tricie, you don't deserve this pain," I say. "You know," Tricie said quietly, "when I left him Thursday afternoon, Trevor said to me, 'I'm gonna hit it out of the park for you, Mommy, so I can bring home the game ball.'" She opens her hand to reveal a tattered baseball. "This was in the seat of the car with him. His coach told me he was given the game ball for scoring a grand slam." She begins to cry again. "He was bringing it to show me, and I can't help but think that if I had gone with him, I could have shared his last happy moment. Oh, God, Taylor, how will I ever forgive myself?" We sit down together and I continue to console her.

After a few moments, she is calmer. She asks, "Have you been here long?" "No, I just got here," I answer. "You were trying to avoid Janny, weren't you?" she asks. "I just didn't want to cause a scene." "Did you really have an affair with Coleman?" she asks. I cry and cover my face, nodding yes. Tricie reaches around my shoulder to hug me. "I always thought you had a crush on him. So, what now? Are you and Joseph going to try to work it out, or will you separate?" "We're separating," I answer sadly.

"Taylor, you've given me advice on love and life so often, and now I'd like to give you some." Tricie takes a deep breath and says, "Andrew loved me like no other man had ever loved me before. He used to tell me that he was lost in a sea of love until he found me, and that he had to work at love until he fell in love with me. Even with all this mess you're in, it's not too late to make things right... It's not too late to have the right kind of love, the kind that doesn't need any work." She squeezes my hand tight. "Thank you, Tricie," I hug her tightly and then stand to leave. "Are you going to stay here?" I ask. "Yes, for a little while... I'm okay; I just need to say goodbye in my own way." I raise my hand to say goodbye and leave her to her thoughts.

10 THE NEXT CHAPTER

In the year that followed my separation from Joseph, I began working as a teacher's aide in a nursery school. It worked out perfectly for Bailey, Dawn, and Joe Jr. because I didn't have to pay for their after-school care. Joseph has full custody of the children. He's been very good about letting me see them as often as I want, although it kills me to bring them back to him.

Just last weekend, Joseph told me that he could understand me wanting to be with the man I really loved; he just couldn't understand why I hadn't told him sooner. He dates occasionally now. Bailey told me she hears girls' voices when she listens to his messages.

Janny moved to Washington State with Jolie. Through Joseph, she has sent me two pictures of Jolie. I have written to her and called her on many different occasions, but not surprisingly she has chosen not to get back in touch with me. Daneka told me that during their last conversation, Janny said she has no interest in talking to me ever again. I miss her.

Daneka left a week ago to begin her studies in South Africa. She also left the United States with a great big diamond ring on her finger. I'm proud of her, not because she's engaged, but because she was smart enough to wait until she was ready.

Tricie went through a really rough period the first couple of months after Andrew and Trevor died, but she and Maya are doing much better now. Tricie founded a group called "Crisis Connection," a support group for parents who survive their children. It has helped her make peace with the loss of Trevor and Andrew.

I hadn't seen Coleman since that night in Janny's house. I didn't asked about him, either, mostly because I didn't know whom to ask. Whenever I thought of him, the same refrain ran through my head: I risked it all only to lose it all.

One Monday morning at work, I was at my desk going over my schedule for the day when one of the aides tapped on my door. "Ms. Salters, there is someone here to see you." "Thanks, Kelly," I said, standing up. As I walked down the hallway I tried to remember if there was a new student starting this morning. I walked up to the front desk and asked our receptionist, "Is someone here waiting for me?" "No," she answered. Confused, I walked out the front doors to look around.

Coleman was standing there with his hands in the pockets of his khaki pants. When he saw me, he hesitantly extended his hand toward me. When I reached for it, he pulled me close to him and studied my expression as if he was trying to read my mind. He then reached up and pushed my hair gently over my shoulder as he said, "I've been waiting so long to see you. I wanted to give you enough time to figure out if you really love me. Did I wait too long?" Without any hesitation, I closed my eyes and pressed my mouth against his ear. "You don't have to wait any more," I whispered.

I had not had the guts to tell Coleman how I really felt about him back when we were teenagers. Instead, I had married a man who loved me wholeheartedly, and and who had ironically given me the strength and courage I needed to go after the man I loved in the same way. This painful year had finally taught me that I don't have to stay in a marriage to be complete, and I don't have to follow other people's standards to achieve my own version of happiness.

One year later, Coleman and I were married quietly on Jefferson Lake, with my children, Jolie, Tricie and Maya in attendance. And I was carrying our first child.

As I stood there with the wind on my face, the sun warming my body, a mature love in my heart, and a new life inside me, I realized how different I was now. The empty feeling was gone. I had learned my lessons about life and love the hard way. I had to lose it all before I could break the cycle I had learned from my parents. I have often wondered why I couldn't have accomplished this with less anguish. Why did my experience have to be so painful for so many? I guess I still have more to learn before I can forgive myself fully, but for now, I gave thanks.

As we embraced after exchanging our vows, I noticed someone walking away in the shadow of the trees. It was Janny! For whatever reason she had come that day. I didn't call out to her; I didn't want to be as selfish as I had been in the past. I just closed my eyes and enjoyed the warmth of the sun and the love I felt for my man.

One of the first orders of business after Coleman and I married was to build us a home. He knew it wouldn't be practical for us to live in his townhouse with the children, and he wanted to design the home we would all feel comfortable in. Because I now had the confidence to ask for what I needed, he built the home of my dreams. Our 6500 square foot, two-story house has a roof that slopes at multiple levels. The four-car garage on the side of the house is behind two elegant arched windows. The façade on the two-story entryway hints at what is inside. The study, which is more for Coleman than me, has built-in cherry wood shelves and is enclosed with beautiful French doors. The family room, kitchen, living room, and master suite all have fireplaces we can gather around. And the kitchen is enormous, but warm and welcoming and with all the latest amenities. It's a room I love spending hours in, alone or with family and friends. The master suite has its own private garden tub and a separate room-sized closet. The house also has a full basement, which Coleman designed especially with the kids in mind. Our home is a practical and comfortable work of art.

My life with Coleman has settled into a healthy rat race. I am finally beginning to feel comfortable about showing my affection to him openly. And with ongoing counseling, I have begun to embrace my imperfections and accept the idea that my life is a work in progress. I have also begun to forgive myself for the disruption I put my family through, although this forgiveness is taking a little more work than the rest.

At my therapist's request, Joseph comes to some of my therapy sessions. He is still the same loving man he has always been, but wiser. He believes his children need to see their parents in a positive working relationship, so he puts his feelings of resentment aside for their sake.

It's Monday morning, and I begin my morning routine just as I have for the last thirteen years. It's my week with the kids, so I rise before them at 5:30 to make their breakfast and pack their lunches. This is also my best time for a little solitude. It's the third Monday of the month, so both Bailey and Dawn have music lessons. Bailey plays cello and Dawn plays flute; no cookie cutter kids in this family!

As I finish preparing breakfast, Coleman makes his way downstairs and into the kitchen holding Daniel, who is now 8½ months old. He greets me with a kiss and, "Good morning love." "Good morning," I answer back, kissing Daniel's chubby cheeks, one of which is still warm from lying on his side. "Are you going to be in town today?" Coleman asks as he reaches for a mug in the cabinet. "Yea, I gotta stop by Music Mania to get a new bag for Bailey's cello. Why?" "Can you pick something up for Jolie? I won't have time." Coleman is putting in long hours on the Revitalization of Downtown Richmond, a multimillion-dollar project that he is very proud to be managing. "Of course – is she coming this weekend?" "Yea, I think so," he answers as I pour hot coffee into his mug and take Daniel from his arms. "Cream?" Coleman shakes his head no.

Coleman and Janny still haven't agreed on a set schedule for Jolie's visits. I understand how Janny's schedule can be, and with her new position in Washington it's even more hectic. Coleman has asked her many times if she can do a little better for his sake – after all, he has an equally demanding, time-consuming and important career. But in true Janny form, no job is as important as hers, and "you can put up bricks and mortar for anyone these days." Janny has perfected the art of demeaning and insulting Coleman, and she has the upper hand in this area.

Bailey is the first to make her way down the steps. I meet her with a kiss and a "Good morning sweetie pie, did you sleep well?" "Yea. It's the thir..." I interrupt, "Third Monday and you've got lessons, I know!" 'My punctual child,' I think as I smile and rub her head. Soon after, Dawn and Joe Jr. make their way into the kitchen. Dawn announces, "Ma, I have lessons today." Coleman smiles at me and says, "You owe me a dollar," for a bet he'd made with me that both girls would come down and announce the exact same thing.

I give kisses to Dawn and Joe Jr. on their foreheads. "Hello Mr. Man, how are you?" I ask Joe Jr.. "Where's my Daddy, Mommy?" This is his first week back from their father's house. Joe Jr. is having the hardest time of the three adjusting to living between two houses. He fusses about not being home with his dad, and usually takes it out on Coleman.

As he usually does, Coleman approaches Joe Jr. hesitantly. "What's going on lil' man?" Joe Jr. turns his back on Coleman. I never allow my children to be rude, so I turn him back around to face Coleman saying, "Someone is speaking to you Joe Jr., and it's very rude to turn your back on him." Joe Jr. crosses his arms and says indignantly, "Nothing!" I gently uncross his arms but don't make a big deal out of his reaction. Knowing that Joe Jr. is unwilling to have a conversation with him right now, Coleman docsn't persist.

The children eat their breakfast while Coleman and I go upstairs to finish our morning routine. Coleman usually leaves the house at 7:00, and I leave at 7:40 to carpool the children to school by 8:00. Joe Jr. now attends Martinique School with his sisters, but Daniel goes with me to the center where I work, which makes my morning commute a whole lot simpler.

Making my way to the front door, I pick up school pencils and snack bags along the way. As I open the front door I notice a car parked in front of the gate, but am distracted corralling the kids. I make my way down the front steps. It isn't until I hear Bailey say, "Hi Aunt Janny!" that I pay full attention. I haven't seen Janny in person since that night in her home. Not knowing what might happen, I hurry the children along; "Bailey, open the door for your sister and brother please, I'll be right there."

I approach Janny uncertainly. She is the first to break the silence. "Hello Taylor." I position Daniel on my hip, "Janny... why are you here? I mean, I wasn't expect..." Janny quickly looks me over and interrupts, "Well, I guess you could say I'm here on business, personal business." "Is everything okay?" I question.

"It's funny that you should ask me that, because I'm here to *make* things okay." I can only stare at her, unsure of where she is going with this. Janny continues, "Time is money, and when I waste time I waste money, so I'll make this very short and very much to the point. You know I never give up anything without a fight. Hell I don't head Chinson Chemical because I have great legs! I'm here to get my husband back." "Oh really," I snarl. "Really. I've decided that I like my family whole, the way it used to be. Coleman may not be the best catch, but he's *my* catch. He and I have discussed me moving back here for a while, or at least until he can find something in Washington."

I smile coyly and walk around to where she is standing. "You've discussed all of this? How long have you been here?" Janny responds with sarcasm, "I'm sorry, you didn't know? I've been here for two weeks now. Don't you and your husband talk in bed? Oh yea, I guess it's kinda hard to talk with your mouth full." Janny turns, gets in her car and drives away.

I hold Daniel tight against my side. I'm confused and angered that I have to question Coleman's actions. Why hadn't he said anything to me? We vowed not to keep secrets anymore.

These thoughts race through my mind as I watch Janny's car until

it is out of sight. I'm startled from my thoughts by Dawn calling

from the car, "Mommy, we're gonna be late." "I'm coming baby."

I spend the better part of this commute trying to decide

whether to call Coleman immediately while he's working, or to

wait until he gets home from work that evening so I can face him

and read his expressions. That will be more telling, I decide, so I

wait. I know I'll be able to learn just as much from his body

language as I do from his words.

I arrive at work early. Now the director of the daycare

center, I've earned an increase in pay that has allowed Joseph to

decrease my alimony, and the scheduling flexibility to spend more

time with my family. I find myself sitting at my desk daydreaming.

I gaze around the room at the pictures of Coleman and me, the

children, and my friends, the evidence of my current life, my

reality. I don't want to imagine there could be anything other than

what I see here, and what I feel; what it appears to be.

I am interrupted by a voice on the intercom: "Mrs. Colebury, there's someone here to see you." "Who is it, Denise?" "It's Ms. Arthur, she responds." "Tell her I'll be right out." I grab my purse and jacket and head out the door. Tricie and her great big smile are just outside to greet me. "Hey girl!" "What's going on Trese? I'll drive," I respond. We walk towards my Suburban. This is just what I need, a simple sweet dose of Tricie.

I don't think she could ever be anyone different, having come from such trying and difficult beginnings. She grew up determined to keep her relationships simple and honest. Beatrice grew up in Connecticut, in a town not far from New York. She and her sister Kelsey were just nine months apart. They were very, very competitive victims of "in-house racism," which was only compounded by the rhetoric from their father Nelson. She and her sister were the products of an interracial marriage. The girls differed significantly in appearance: Beatrice has a skin tone somewhere between the shades of their mother and father, dirty blonde hair with a very silky texture and bright blue eyes like their mother; whereas Kelsey has the same skin tone, thick textured hair and brown eyes as their father. This should have meant nothing, but in the Arthur home it meant everything.

Beatrice's parents were wealthy and successful; Carrie Arthur was a professor at Yale University and Nelson was the owner of Nelson Bank and Trust. They lived in an upscale community, and the girls grew up playing golf at the country club with their father, having high tea every Sunday after church with their friends, taking piano lessons, and attending the finest private school in the state. Nelson preached to his children about his difficult childhood and reminded them almost daily of how difficult his upbringing had been as a black man. He often said that the fact that they were "half and half" made them 50 percent closer to an easier life. Sadly, he also set them up to compete with each other by telling them repeatedly that it would be easier for Tricie because of her blue eyes and looks, and that Kelsey would have to work harder to get ahead.

When the girls were young, Carrie did all she could to keep them close and levelheaded. She told them that they were equally beautiful in the worlds' eyes, and that their differences reflected the mixing of the beauty of both their parents. For a while this was enough, and the girls remained immune to the idea that either of them was better than the other. Eventually, though, their father's words overshadowed their mother's and the competition between the two began in earnest.

Kelsey focused all of her jealousy and pain on her schoolwork and sports until she surpassed her sister in achievements. She hoped this would gain her father's equal affection. Instead, he continued to favor his 'blue-eyed girl,' which only made Kelsey more determined to take her sister down.

Unfortunately, Beatrice began to embrace Nelson's rhetoric as she approached adulthood. She eventually decided that she was prettier and smarter than Kelsey, and even though her sister's talents were superior, she believed her own physical attributes would take her farther. Beatrice's blind trust in these ideas left her oblivious to her sister's conniving ways. She was unaware that Kelsey had carried on an affair with her husband until it was too late for all of them.

There is one good thing that has come from this. Although my friend has been deeply wounded, for most of her life and by those closest to her, it has taught her to be more mindful about the people in her life. Tricie can be a real pain in the ass with her self-righteous ways at times. But she is just like the rest of us: imperfect and lovable all at once. I love her to pieces.

In the car, Tricie makes small talk. "Oh yea, I've been meaning to tell you that next month, the Crisis Connection is going to have its First Annual Walk for Life. Are you going to come?" "You know it!" I say. "And I talked to Daneka on Sunday," she continues. "She's coming back stateside on Friday the fourth, so I was thinking of scheduling the walk for the week after she arrives, so she can get over her jet lag... are you following me, Taylor?"

Not aware of my blank expression, I apologize, "I'm sorry Trese. You are not going to believe what happened this morning." "What?" Tricie asks while looking down and adjusting her shirt. "I walk out my front door, and who's standing there but Janny!" "Get the fuck out!" she yells. "I kid you not, and wait a minute, that's not the best part – she goes on to tell me that she wants Coleman back, and that she's been here for two weeks now to make that happen." "My God Taylor, do you think she's serious?"

I pull into the parking lot of the restaurant and park the car. I turn to face Tricie and say flatly, "Tricie, you know Janny just as well as I do, and you know she's not one to bullshit. Of course she means it! I'm just pissed off that Coleman didn't say anything to me. He asked me this morning to pick up something for Jolie, but that was it. I'm floored." Tricie asks, "What are you worried about Taylor? Do you think that Coleman would actually leave the family he has made with you to go back to Janny? He never loved her, you know that as a fact." "I don't know Trese, maybe he just wants to go back to what's familiar to him," I say doubtfully. "That's crap, Taylor, and you know it. Relax, things will work out. They always do. I'm optimistic!" We finally exit the car and walk arm-in-arm into the restaurant.

That evening I'm rushing around cleaning up the early morning mess that I didn't get around to. Coleman usually gets home between 6.15 and 6:30, and it's now 7:10. With my early morning encounter with Janny still on my mind, I can feel myself becoming furious. As the evening progresses I'm distracted with feeding the kids, helping them finish up homework, and getting them into bed. Finally I get into the shower. I haven't been in for five minutes when I hear Coleman enter the house. His footsteps slowly come up the stairs and finally enter the bathroom. My back is turned to him, and I'm waiting to hear what he has to say. Coleman breaks the silence. "Taylor, I'm sorry I'm so late." I quietly respond, "We'll talk when I get out, Coleman." Why am I disappointed at his admission of being late? Because I really wanted him to come in and spill the beans about everything I already knew. I hoped he would come into the bathroom and tell me that Janny was here, wanted him back, and that there was no way in hell he would ever leave me, his beloved wife. But that didn't happen.

I get out of the shower and walk into the bedroom. Coleman is standing in front of the walk-in closet, removing his shirt and tie. I get directly to the point. "Is there something you want to talk to me about?" Coleman quickly answers back "No, should there be?" "Gee, I don't know. Would you say your ex-wife being in town and showing up at our doorstep this morning to tell me that she wants you back is something to talk about?" I query sarcastically, throwing my towel on the bed and slumping down.

Coleman's body language changes immediately. He turns to face me and explains, "I'm sorry Taylor, I didn't know how to tell you that, but it's not what you're thinking." "How do you even know what I'm thinking? Why don't you tell me what this is about, Coleman? Why is she really here?" Coleman begins to explain, "A couple of months ago, Janny..." I rise to my feet, furious. "A COUPLE OF MONTHS AGO?!" Coleman reaches out to grab my arm. "Wait a minute Taylor, let me finish. She told me she wanted to talk about sharing custody, and to do that she needed come over here to find a good school for Jolie. She also said that I would have to pay half the tuition, which is fine by me. Taylor, you know how badly I've wanted to share custody of Jolie. But when she got here, things changed. She started telling me how Jolie needed her father around – that she couldn't grow to be a strong young woman without the support of her father. She also said that she could probably work on this coast in order to give Jolie the stability she needs."

This is all too much. My mind is racing. I begin to walk away in anger but then I turn to him and ask, "Are you kidding me Coleman? Do you actually believe that shit?" "You know that she has the upper hand in this, Taylor." "Yeah right, Coleman, and she wants to take that same hand and dig a little deeper into the pot. Did you hear me when I said that she told me she wants you back? And not even because she loves you, but because it was a matter of *not* losing to me! You're still just a door prize to her."

"And what am I to you Taylor – have you figured that out yet? Am I property? Or maybe a consolation prize?" I am shocked and bewildered by his question, and at a loss for words. Defeated by it all, I'm silent. Coleman grabs the blanket and goes into the den to sleep for the night.

I am now face-to-face with one of my biggest fears: that Coleman may feel he made a mistake leaving Janny for me. I know in my heart that I made the right decision. I love Coleman, in a way I never thought I could love. I'm stronger because of it, and if I had to I could handle being without him. I just don't want to.

The following morning, I awaken to the sound of my alarm clock. I squirm across the bed to quickly shut it off before it wakes the baby, and realize that Coleman never came back to bed. I get up and grab my robe, tie it around my waist and make my way downstairs. To my surprise, Coleman is sitting in the kitchen at the table. He looks disheveled; his hair is messy and his eyes are red. I stop in the doorway and we look at one another. I'm not good at grudges, so I carefully break the silence, "I'm sorry, I'm sorry for not trusting that you would make the right decision." He immediately jumps in, "I should've told you she was in town Taylor. I apologize for not doing that, it made the whole situation look shady." Coleman stands up and embraces me there in the doorway. He cups my face between both his hands, then presses my head against his chest. "I love you so much Taylor. I will never do anything to lose you – I mean that." I believe my husband.

11 CONSEQUENCES

About once a month now, my Saturdays are "Tricie days,"
meaning I somehow have agreed to be connected to Beatrice's hip
and accompany her on all of her errands. She volunteers at the
Mission of Hope Center and afterwards she holds her group
meetings for the Crisis Connection.

When Trevor and Andrew first died, she needed me there
for emotional support. Now I go because she's become accustomed
to my presence, and because we reward ourselves with shoe
shopping afterwards (a great incentive for any girl!). This
particular Saturday, I get up a bit earlier than usual to squeeze in a
bike ride before we meet.

Soon after Coleman and I married I started riding again. I hadn't realized how much I had missed the solace of the back trails: the sounds, smells, and wind on my face were vital to my mental health and therapeutic in many ways. I don't have to share this time with anyone, and whatever my reflections are as I ride, I can think with no interruptions.

I slip out of bed and into the bathroom. Coleman designed our bathroom with my preferences in mind, but I've noticed that he enjoys this bathroom's perks as much as I do. In this bathroom, the triple-headed shower, encased in clear plate glass, is centered in the room. To the right is a double sink with two separate oval mirrors. The toilet is concealed by a partition in the right corner. To the left of the shower, and sunken down two steps, is the whirlpool bath encased in stone, with skylights overhead to allow daylight to cascade down from above. I quietly turn on the left showerhead and step in to lather up. Soon, I feel Coleman slide in behind me. Startled at first, I turn around to face him, "I thought you were asleep." Coleman wraps his arms around my back and pulls on my hair from behind to wet my hair and face, and begins caressing my arms as he kisses and licks the water off my neck. He grabs my ass with both hands, pulling me toward him to slide his erect penis between my legs. I lift my left leg and wrap it around his right one as he kisses down my neck and across my chest. In one swift movement he lifts me up to his waist to get a mouthful of breast. I fold my legs tightly around his back, locking them behind him. I grab the bars on each side of the shower walls to support myself, smiling as I remember our designer asking Coleman why he would want two bars up so high. I gracefully lower myself, allowing my wet body to slide against Coleman's. He holds me tight, keeping my body close to his. I grab fistfuls of his wet curly hair and bring his mouth to mine, taking passionate mouthfuls of his tongue. Coleman lowers himself to his knees as his hand presses me firmly against the wall. He glances up at me with a coy slanted smile, and I return the smile, saying, "You're going to make me late." He lifts my leg, drapes it on his shoulder and gently kisses around my pussy, saying, "I'm going to make you feel good." I use both hands to brace myself against the shower walls. Coleman licks around my clit, then with his mouth covering the opening completely, slides his tongue between my pussy lips. He uses his hands cupped over my ass to press my mound close to his face, not wanting to miss a single drop. He continues this tongue caress, matching my rhythmic body movements with just the right speed, not too quick or too slow. Sensing that I am close to climaxing, he rises to his feet, pinching both nipples between his fingers. He raises my leg again, bracing it against his body, and slides his dick into my soaking wet channel. I dip my head into Coleman's chest and gasp with pleasure as we fuck with slow measured strokes. I quietly moan and reach up to shove my finger into Coleman's mouth. He speeds up, also approaching climax, and is panting. I whisper in his ear "I want you to come in my mouth." This always pushes him into ecstasy. He pulls out as I drop to my knees and take Coleman fully into my mouth, matching and balancing his strokes with my mouth and tongue. Suddenly he grips the back of my head, and with a deep guttural groan, climaxes deep in my mouth. Breathing very quickly and heavily, he lifts me up to my feet and kisses me intensely. He laughs, "Girl, you can make a brotha week at the fuckin' knees."

Needless to say, I am very late. I find myself rushing through the park, looking for Tricie. It is now 11:00 and I was supposed to meet her an hour ago! Tricie is sitting on a park bench by the pond. I hurry to her, and out of breath I say, "Trese, I'm sorry, I left you a message... did you get it?" "I got it." Tricie stands up and we begin to walk over to the Mission for Hope Center. Tricie looks me over, noticing my hair, which I'd pulled into a ponytail while it was still dripping wet in the back. "Nice long shower huh?" she remarks. I smile, wrap my arm around her and say, "I love you, sweetie, don't be mad okay?" "Oh, I'm not mad at you, I'm mad at Coleman for being so damn horny in the morning!" We laugh.

After we serve soup at the Mission Center, and Tricie concludes her meeting with the Crisis Connection support group, she finds me dozing on the couch in the hallway. My busy days often get the best of me and I don't realize how exhausted I am. Tricie sits down beside me, which startles me awake. I glance at my watch and ask, "How did it go?" Tricie, in a dispirited tone admits, "Okay, but toward the end I started to think about how two years ago things were so wonderful and so complete, in my own family and with all of you guys. I hate these broken circles, ya know?"

I know what she means, and I know what she wants. I grab her hand and ask, "Do you blame me?" "No, I don't blame you Taylor. I just wish we could all be back together like we used to be." On cue, we look away from each other. I think she may feel guilty for asking me, and I feel guilty for being the cause of the separation. Either way, there is no simple answer and definitely no quick fix.

I turn back to Tricie and break the silence with, "The Crisis Connection walk is scheduled for next Saturday at 3:00, right? And doesn't Daneka's flight come in on Friday at 6:00 in the evening? I told her we'd both pick her up." "Cool," Tricie says, then continues, "I also talked to Janny last night." I try to sound neutral as I say, "That's good." "She told me she wants Coleman back." I jerked my head in Tricie's direction, shaking it in defiance. "She told *you*?" "Yea, she said that Jolie needs her father." I am shocked, and I can't tell where Tricie plans to go with the rest of this conversation. I remain silent. "Taylor, are you mad at me for talking to her about that?" I stand, and trying not to sound too angry, I lie. "Never, Trese. It's just that this whole situation is so fucked up. What am I supposed to say? Who the hell should I get mad at? My ex-best friend, whose ex-husband I had an affair with, for wanting him back now that he's my husband?! This is a goddamned excruciating joke!" People in the hallway begin to look in our direction. Tricie pulls on my arm to sit me back down on the couch. "How about some deep cleansing breaths, soldier?" Tricie jokes, and then suggests, "Let's go get a drink." I look down at my watch thinking to myself, 'it must be five o'clock somewhere!' "It's only 1:30 in the afternoon." "I know, so let's make it a double!" I smile, and we both stand and walk out of the building.

We do make it doubles, a couple of them. Later, as I pull into into my driveway, I see Coleman in the yard playing with Daniel and Joe Jr.. His knees muddy from crawling around on the grass, Joe Jr. is running and jumping, looking happier than usual, which makes me think to myself, 'I'm so lucky to have a second chance with a prince, so I'll fight tooth and nail to keep him.'

Later that evening I meet with Joseph to discuss the upcoming holidays and how we'll split our time with the kids. After we make the plans, we typically discuss them with the kids to make sure they are okay with them. Joseph has consistently stepped up to the plate in favor of harmony. He is the same great father he's always been, always focused on what is good for his family. I even notice he's beginning to do good things for himself: traveling, and spending afternoons doing things he enjoys. Although it isn't in his nature to care for himself first, he has embraced the familial trickle-down theory, meaning that if he takes care of the things around him, he is also taking care of himself.

We usually meet at Benny's restaurant when we need to talk. It's central for both of us. As I pull into the parking lot I notice Joseph's car and pull into the space beside it. I flip down the mirror to brush the hair off my shoulders and get out of the car. As I walk in, I notice Joseph standing in the hallway. He is wearing a charcoal gray fitted sweater and a pair of black khakis. Handsome as ever. He waves to me as I approach the door. "How's it going

Taylor?" he asks, while opening the door. "Good, Joseph." he

places his hand at the small of my back to lead me to our table.

First I sit, then Joseph does. As I settle into my seat Joseph

continues, "How are the kids doing?" "Joe Jr. is better this week,

and all in all, they're doing okay. Changing the subject, I ask, "Are

you going to make it to therapy on Wednesday?" "Of course,"

Joseph agrees. He continues, "I also need to ask if the kids can stay

with you this weekend. I have to go to Arizona Thursday, Friday

and Saturday, and I won't get back until late Sunday." "Sure."

"Thanks," Joseph continues, "I'll pick them up tomorrow for

dinner and tell them all about it then." "Sounds good."

The waiter approaches the table. "Welcome, may I start

you with something to drink? A glass of wine or a cocktail

perhaps?" Joseph motions his hand to me, "No drink for me, I'm

actually ready to order. I'll have the smoked salmon with a side

salad, no dressing, just a lemon please." "And for you, sir?" "I'll

have the same, with Thousand Island dressing." "Something from

the bar for you, sir?" Joseph again turns to me and asks, "You sure you don't want a drink?" I confirm, and Joseph orders a Guinness. The waiter takes the menus and leaves us.

Joseph continues his small talk, keeping everything straightforward and direct. "I was thinking about putting the house on the market. Is that okay?" "Yeah, that's fine." "I feel like I should get something smaller, you know? That big-ass kitchen was never my idea." He smiles a half smile as the waiter delivers his beer. I add, "Dawn was picked to play in the fall concert on the 12th; can you make it?" "Of course." Joseph pulls out his day planner. "Shit, what time on the 12th?" "6:00." "Okay, that's good." He marks it in his book.

Trying to keep the conversation going, I carefully mention, "Coleman has Jolie that weekend." I study his face, wondering if this information is welcome or not. Joseph sips his beer as I continue, "He wants to bring her along." Joseph finishes his gulp, puts the glass down then places both hands on the table. He waits a moment before asking me, "What are you waiting for me to say to that? That I can't wait, or some crazy bullshit like that?" "No, but at some point you do need to understand that all the kids are going to see all of us adults together, and whether we like it or not, we need to make that work." Joseph interjects, "No, *you* need for that to work, Taylor. You chose to take this boat ride, but that doesn't guarantee you smooth sailing!" He sits back in his chair, finishes the first Guinness and signals for another. An awkward silence settles between us. I hate how I've made this, how things are and how much effort every little thing now takes. "Joe, you know this is *not* about me. If it makes you feel better, I won't go, or I'll sit in the back. It doesn't matter. But Coleman is my husband now. Yes, I have taken this boat ride, so I can't keep denying him when he tries to play a part in our children's lives."

Joseph doesn't answer. Sipping the foam off his new beer, he stares away blankly. "I'll get back to you on that one." Joseph is giving in. I know he's not happy. The only reason he submits is for his children, and maybe a little for me. Am I taking advantage of that? He stretches his arms out, smirks and laughs to himself. "What?" I ask, half knowing what he's thinking. "I was just thinking that if anyone had told me on the day I got married that my wife would leave me for my best friend, I would've looked at them like they were on crack." "Joe, I didn't mean for this to go this way." The waiter brings their meals to the table. "You know what, pack mine to go." Joseph pulls out his wallet and drops a $100.00 bill on the table. "Enjoy your dinner, Taylor." Joe finishes his beer, gets up and walks out. The waiter, startled, asks me, "Ma'am, would you like yours wrapped as well?" "No, but I will have a glass of white wine." As the waiter turns to walk away, I call him back. "Actually, I'll have a gin and tonic." I sit across from Joe's empty chair, his wrapped meal and the empty beer glass. I want to cry, to feel sorry for myself, and to punish myself because it's what I deserve. So I finish my drink and eat my meal quietly and alone, with only my self-pity for company.

I arrive at home not long after and park in the driveway. I turn the car off and sit there for a moment, to prepare myself for the next stress. I still have Janny on my mind and am worried about what she is up to. I unlock the front door and find Coleman sitting on the couch with the kids spread out all around him. Hearing me enter, he looks back and says, "Hey love." "Hi sweetheart, hi babies!" The kids run up to me, hugging my legs.

Joe Jr. pulls on my arm and I pick him up. He asks, "Where's my Daddy?" "Daddy went home big boy, but he told me to give you something." "What?" I kiss him on the cheek and tickle his tummy, and Joe Jr. laughs and squiggles out of my arms. Bailey then takes her turn at me. "Mom, I'm going to Ashland on a field trip on the 29th. Are you gonna come?" "I'm not sure Bailey, let me see if I can get the day off. Who's your second choice if I can't?" She turns to Coleman and asks, "Cole, can you come if my Mom can't?" "Absolutely!" Coleman looks at me and shrugs his shoulders as if to say 'Go figure!' Dawn then asks, "Mom, did you tell Daddy about my concert on the 12th? Is he going to be here?" I hesitate, not knowing how to answer. Joe's been so good at keeping his children separate from the discontent he has with me, but the way he left this evening, I'm hoping his sentiment isn't changing. "Daddy is going to get back to me on that one puddin' pie." I sit down on the couch beside Coleman.

"What happened at dinner?" he whispers into my ear. I quietly respond, "Well, let's just say it happened." "You want to talk?" "No, not now. I may ask you for a listening ear later, but not now." Coleman turns my face toward his and gently follows its outline with his finger. He strokes my jaw, and then rubbing his finger across my bottom lip, he kisses it. "I love you so much Taylor, you're my everything. Please remember that you're not alone in all of this."

Coleman is a remarkably sensitive man. I love the way he recognizes when I'm struggling and catches me with his strong arms when I fall. Coleman brings me joy with my breakfasts in bed; he takes my angst away when he massages my feet; he soothes my fears while rubbing my back in the bath. He tells me that he has waited all these years for the woman he really loves, and now that he has me, he wants to make up for lost time. No one would guess when looking at his imposing masculine frame that he can be so sympathetic and sensitive to a woman's needs.

Coleman presses his mouth to my ear and whispers, "I guess I'll have to give you something to smile about tonight." I smile back at him and kiss his lips. He gets up and goes go to the kitchen, returning with a glass of my favorite Chardonnay. We all sit together and watch the rest of the movie the kids were watching when I came in.

Later that night I go through my normal nighttime routine with the kids. I think about how I sometimes miss being at home with them full-time. I know that Coleman would support me if I decided to stay home again. But for now, working offers me a mental break and financial benefits.

In bed that night, I wait to see if Coleman will bring up anything about Janny. I can sense that it's on his mind. I lie on my belly across the end of the bed to read, wearing Coleman's t-shirt and panties. Coleman is lying beside me in his shorts, maintaining contact by rubbing my thigh while he watches a basketball game. "Janny left to go back home this morning." "Really?" "Yea, Jolie called me with her cell phone to tell me that Mommy was getting tired of the Virginia air and couldn't wait to get back home." I wait for more, then put my book down and look over at Coleman to read his expression. He continues, "She did say that Jolie can spend Thanksgiving and New Years with me, but she wants her for Christmas." "That's good Cole, at least she's offering a compromise." "I just wish she'd understand that I love my daughter all the time, not just when we are on good terms," he says sadly. I try to listen to Coleman's concerns about Jolie, but I can't stop Janny's voice in the back of my mind saying she wants Coleman back.

To keep the peace tonight, I choose not to ask more about Janny right then, but I'm wondering why she left and it's really eating at me. The Janny I know would not leave loose ends, ever, and if she goes so far as to say something threatening, she damned sure means it. In that moment, I decide to drop it. If Janny is gone, that's good, at least for now.

Friday evening arrives sooner than expected. Coleman is ready for a busy evening alone with the kids. He loves being a father. Joseph loved being a father too, but I'm especially proud to see Coleman putting so much effort into loving my children when the odds have been stacked against him. It makes his position as a dad to this group all the more difficult, but his effort is starting to pay off.

I leave work early to spend a little time with the kids, and then say my goodbyes. I grab a bagel, tuck a banana under my chin, and head out the door. I take Coleman's Volvo and leave him the Suburban, since he has all the kids. Tricie is standing in front of Demerick's Ballet School when I pull up. She steps up to my front passenger window and instructs, "Follow me home so that I can drop my car off." I mockingly salute and wait for her to pull her car around. When we get to Tricie's house, she runs in to drop off her bags and rushes back out the front door. It's only 3:31 – phew! For once, we are making good time.

On the way to the airport, we both enjoy the scenery of hillsides full of trees with leaves in glorious colors. We chat about past day trips we've taken together, and the ones we plan to take with Daneka later in the year. We've both been missing her outspokenness. She has always been the 'mouth' in our circle of friends; the one we all count on to be honest, no matter what.

We also want to hear more about her new fiancé, Melvin Graham. He is just a name to us at this point, and without more details we can't decide whether to rip him to shreds or welcome him with open arms. Danny doesn't say much about him, but that's just her way. She is reserved, especially about the things that are important to her, and about matters of her heart.

We arrive at the airport in record time, especially for a Friday during rush hour! We park the car and make our way through the airport. At the arrival gate, we join the crowd of waiting people, jutting our heads back and forth and peering through the plate glass windows. Daneka's flight lands right on time at 6:00. Like two little girls waiting for their parents, we stand there holding hands, searching beyond the passengers leaving the plane in single file. Finally, we see Daneka, dressed in a long African robe. Her braids, which now seem to be twice as long, are cascading down her back. She looks beautiful. Her dark brown skin is radiant, and her bright smile can be seen even from this distance. When she spots us, her normal gait becomes a sprint. We wend our way through the crowd to meet her halfway, and she drops her bags and jumps into our arms for a three-way love fest.

We hug, kiss and cry in that very spot for what seems like hours. When we finally pull away from each other, Daneka is naturally the first to speak. "Wassup girls?" She steps back at bit. "Let me look at you guys. Beatrice, you finally cut that mess I see..." She remarks while rubbing her hands through Tricie's hair. "Whatever, Dan," Tricie says as she pulls Daneka's hand from her head. "And Taylor, I love *your* hair this length. You're not trying to lose weight are you?" "No girl, but I'm still breastfeeding," I tell her, placing both my hands over my stomach. "Let's roll! I'm so happy to see this city again that I don't know what to do with myself!"

The three of us walk arm-in-arm to my car, barely letting one another get a word in edgewise. But on the ride home we slow things down so that we can listen to Daneka as she tells us about her trip to Africa and her fiancé. "Damn, I miss showers, real ones, and French fries, and really good music." "Are you kidding me? Ms. African pride over here? We've been worried about how long you're going to stay in the States before you go back," Tricie teases. Daneka continues "Don't get me wrong, I love the people, *my* people, but I've learned that I'm so Americanized, I can't live there!"

Having had enough small talk, I decide to ask, "Hey, you never sent us a picture of Melvin or anything – what's up with that?" "He's the bomb, Taylor, you're gonna love him! He's like a chocolate chip cookie, yummy! And he just came back a couple of days ago, so you'll get to meet him soon enough." "Good," I say, "That gives me an excuse to have everyone over for dinner." Daneka continues, "That'd be great. I want you all to meet him. Janny loves him."

Tricie squints one eye, tilts her head and asks, "What do you mean, 'Janny loves him'? When did she meet him?" A bit nervous, Daneka straightens her skirt, looks away and says, "She came out a few times. Short visits, of course. I mean, you know Janny doesn't like heat, and crowds of black folks, not the *real* ones anyway. I don't know why she thinks she can escape all of that in Africa... that home girl cracks me up!" I smile an awkward smile while Daneka continues, "She kept giving me these ridiculous tasks, like looking for which hotels had pool views and in-room Jacuzzis! When's the last time you guys spoke to her?"

We endure another even longer silence. Daneka turns to look at Tricie in the back seat, and then looks back at me. Tricie breaks the silence. "She stayed at my place just last weekend." "What about you, Tay?" I don't say anything. I can't. Daneka uses the opportunity to lecture; "Sooo, does the absence of a response mean you haven't been working on making things right between you two? ...Hello?" I love Danny. She is the voice of truth, the 'no excuse for what I did.' She knows me far too well, so I can't bullshit her, and I don't want to. I just want to enjoy this time with my friend, and not have to deal with that unspoken truth. But I do.

I sit up in my seat and try to explain; "Daneka, believe me, I know the wrong I've done to our friendship..." "Umm, no shit, Tay. But I believe we've discussed the concept of *friend ownership* before..." Daneka retorts. I sigh, smirk and continue, "We have, and that's why I haven't been in touch with her. I tried to connect early on, I really did, but all of my letters came back unopened. All I ever received from her were pictures of Jolie, and that was through Joseph."

Now comes awkward silence number three. At this rate, I should probably stop counting. Realizing I can't avoid the subject, I break the ice. "I saw Janny the other day." "Really? How did that go?" "Well, she came by specifically to tell me that she wants Coleman back." "What goes around comes around," Daneka digs. "Yea, I know, and it takes two to tango, too. You wanna throw any more clichés in here?" Tricie interrupts, "C'mon, c'mon guys, let's not do this. What's happened has happened. Either we get through this or we don't, but if there's anything we do agree on, it's that we all love each other, and we all want the best from a situation that is not the best right now... Hell, I don't know if it ever will be."

Daneka waits a moment. She knows that Trese is right. While she hates what I've done, she loves me, and accepting a piss-poor situation is not Daneka's strength. But she leans over and kisses me on the cheek, then leans over the back seat and grabs Tricie's hand. "Who'd have ever thought that Tricie would become the voice of reason?" We decide to lighten the mood and have that good ol' girl talk we do so well, for the rest of the ride.

I drop them both off at Tricie's house. Although Daneka typically stays at my house, she says she's too tired to put on the game face she needs to deal with Coleman. I understand only too well why she doesn't want to stay with me. I now have one more chip to add to my "you fucked up" pile. I'm making my friends avoid me in order to maintain their own level of acceptance and peace. I smile and wave as they both go into the house, but as I pull away I finally let go. I cry from deep in my gut as I make my way home.

At home, I tiptoe up the stairs, stopping to peek into the kids' rooms. Daniel and Joe Jr. are sound asleep. Bailey and Dawn have once again made it into the same bed. I pull the covers up over them, lean over and kiss their heads, noticing that baby smell that evokes the sweetest of emotions every single time. I stand and gaze across their room, enjoying the tranquility. It's wonderful to be in the midst of that serenity. I quietly close their door and make my way into our bedroom. Coleman makes me smile; he is fast asleep and the TV is still on. I back into the corner and quietly take my clothes off before slipping naked into bed with him and aligning my body with his.

Coleman slowly begins to awaken from the feeling of my body against him. He reaches back to hold me close, then rolls over, wraps his arms around me and kisses me nimbly on the lips. "Mmmm, how was the drive?" He runs his hands through my hair. "Good," I answer, using the remote to turn the TV off and dim the light above us. I kiss him back. "And how was Ms. Daneka, with her sassy self? Did she turn into one of the other sistas in the muthaland?" he asks affectionately. "You know Daneka. She looks beautiful, and she seems happy to be home."

Coleman, now more awake, pulls his head back to study my face, as he always does, as if he never wants to forget each part. He inspects the curve of my nose, the roundness of my cheeks, the incline of my eyes and the ampleness of my lips, as if they are brand new to him. "Look at my baby, just look at you." I smile, from the same part of my gut that brought tears earlier. He pulls me on top of his warm body, and we make heartfelt, passionate love.

12 THE CIRCLE'S STILL BROKEN

It's early Saturday morning. Coleman awakens to Dawn

standing beside him with Daniel in her arms, pulling at his sleeve.

"Coleman, baby Daniel has teeth coming in, you wanna see?"

Coleman reaches across to make sure that both of our bare bodies

are covered with the sheet. "Show me, sweet pea." Dawn proceeds

to pry Daniel's mouth open and reveals a lonely tooth breaking

through his gums. "I'll bet he wants to use that tooth too, huh?" "I

think so," Dawn smiles a coy smile. "Okay baby, take him to your

room and I'll make you guys something to eat okay?" "Yes sir,"

Dawn answers and leaves the room carrying Daniel, his legs

dangling between hers.

Coleman rolls across me and kisses my ear lobe, startling me. I begin to stir. "Nuh-uh, don't wake up love, I'm gonna make you something to eat." I simper, close my eyes and fall back to sleep, only to be awakened in what seems like two short minutes by Bailey and Joe Jr. jumping into the bed with me. "Mom, can we go to Paradise Park today?" Wanting to pacify them quickly, I agree, "yes, yes we can." I reach around, hugging Bailey closely around her neck. Joe Jr. takes that opportunity to plant himself between my legs, remote in hand, searching for his favorite channel. Coleman comes in, carrying a tray full of warm bagels with strawberry cream cheese for us all to share. Breakfast is served!

Sitting here with my family all together, with all the noise and in what some might see as absolute chaos, I think about my parents. Did they ever experience this feeling of joy that I have now? In all of this lovely domestic confusion, had they found solace and joy in one another? I hoped that they had at some point.

In the past few years, my mother has been suffering from dementia and my dad's been struggling to care for her. At the start of this past year he finally had to move her into a nursing home where she can receive around-the-clock care.

My sister has been dealing with her own set of hurdles. She recently told her husband to get treatment for his addictions, letting him know that if he didn't, she would pursue life on her own. This is an amazing and utterly fortuitous thing to see from her. Her husband tried to convince her that being with his family was all the therapy he needed, but in the end he did exactly what she asked. He committed himself to a yearlong rehabilitation program. I know better than to get involved in this situation. I love my sister and will be at her side in an instant if she asks, but I can tell by her comments that she wants to do this on her own. The best thing I can do for her at this juncture is to respect her wishes.

Besides, my own ship is beginning to take on water from its family issues. From what I know of Coleman's family so far, they are very practical, common-sense people, and as folksy as a Norman Rockwell painting. His mother was born in Portugal and still speaks her native tongue. His father is Jamaican, minus the dreads but with the full lilting, rhythmic accent. Coleman's physical features are a masculine version of his mother's. His mother is overprotective of her only child, and is therefore unhappy with all of the women in his life, including Janny and me. Her granddaughter Jolie is the exception, of course.

Coleman is looking forward to having Jolie for the coming weekend because it's her birthday. We feel that a party is in order, and I'm hoping it will be complete with grandparents and all the people who love her. Coleman and I decide that we should invite Janice and Joseph to join the party, so Coleman makes the call to Janny and I call Joseph.

Janice says that she can't come. She is leaving the following morning for Tokyo and will be gone through the following week. She says she'll be taking Jolie shopping in Manhattan the day she returns, and then Jolie will fly home to Virginia later that evening with their au pair. I don't know of any other 12-year-old on the planet who does as much traveling as Jolie! And with the recent changes, I can see it taking a toll on her. I stay silent about it, however. I remind myself that Coleman and Janny need to figure out co-parenting in their own way. Still, it's hard for me to sit back at this point. Before Coleman and I were "us" I had loved Jolie as my adopted niece; now I've switched gears and am beginning to love her as a daughter.

When I call Joseph, he also says that he has other plans. I can't remember what the plans are because I'm disappointed and am not listening intently once he declines. I expect that all my other friends will be in attendance, though, (I know that Tricie will bring Maya and Daneka will bring Melvin), so I arrange to have an adult menu as well as one for the kids. Coleman has also invited a few of his friends and their children, so we'll have a good crowd for a great celebration.

Entertaining is my gig, and I always take joy in it. The thought that a potentially stressful situation could arise from this get together doesn't even occur to me; I am simply looking forward to celebrating with Jolie and our friends and family.

Our babysitter Kate and her best friend arrive at about 9:15 a.m. the morning of Jolie's party to pick up the kids. She has been working for us for the last five months, and already has an excellent rapport with them. "Good morning Kate." "Hey Ms.

Colebury, you remember Moiré right?" I dry my wet hands on the back of my sweatpants and reach out to shake Moiré's hand, "Of course I do, good to see you Moiré." Kate is surprised that the children are ready and waiting. "I see they're all ready – my goodness, I don't know how you do it!" Kate exclaims. "Practice makes perfect, Kate," I say with a smile. "So, what are the plans?" "Well, I thought we'd go to the science museum, have some lunch, and then go ice skating." "Good deal!" I agree as I hand Kate my car keys and credit card. "You guys get a nice lunch too, okay? And can you have them back at 4:30?" "Absolutely." Kate promises. The two girls then take Bailey, Dawn, Joe Jr. and Daniel out the door.

I spend most of the day on the phone tightening up loose ends. So far, so good. I know Jolie loves Winnie the Pooh, so I have 150 helium-filled Winnie the Pooh balloons with streamers delivered, and let a bunch go in every room in the house so the streamers hang from the ceilings. I confirm the order of a square white tower cake with strawberry filling, her favorite, from our neighborhood bakery. The cake feeds 75 people and should be imposing enough to delight any young girl (I know full well that

kids are impressed by size!). For the adults, I have three different

dishes: grilled chicken with roasted red tomatoes, mushrooms,

olives and red onions over linguini; spaghetti and meatballs with

Italian sausage topped with parmesan cheese; and finally, platters

of sliced roast pork, beef and turkey with large baskets of fresh

Italian bread. I have also prepared a green salad with breadcrumbs

and homemade dressing.

Coleman leaves in the late morning to pick up Taylor's gift

and the sodas, wine, beer and ice. I stay at the house to wait for my

parents, who are invited as well. True to form, my father calls to

cancel. No surprise there. Then Coleman's parents call and

promise to be here by 5:00. It's my hope to cut the cake by 6:00, in

a perfect world anyway. By 3:00 I have finished decorating and

have set up the gift table and the buffet table. All that is left is to

get myself ready.

Coleman arrives, dropping things as he makes his way

down the hallway. Hearing the commotion, I rush downstairs to

help. Our eyes meet briefly and I smile, taking the ice and the grocery bags from his left hand. "I got it Cole." "Thanks. Did my Mom call?" "Yea, this morning around 11:00 or so. She said they'd be here by 5:00."

Coleman places the remaining bags on the counter, and once he has his hands free, he turns to embrace me. I wrap my arms around his neck and kiss him on the mouth. "So that means, if my calculations are correct, we have about an hour to spare," he smirks while raising my arms above my head to remove my shirt. "My God, you never get enough, do you?" I ask. He pulls down at the front of my bra to release a breast so he can nibble on it. "Of you? Never!" He kisses my neck, around my ears and back to my mouth. He then steps away from me while holding my hands out to each side and says, "I just like looking at you." I smile, feeling slightly bashful. Before I can continue that thought, he scoops me up into his arms and carries me upstairs.

Standing in front of the mirror a little while later, I finish up my makeup and review my choice of clothing. A powder blue deep V-neck shirt, a pair of black fitted flood pants and simple black slides; I'm going for a casual-but-charming look. I decide to wear my hair down and parted in the middle, even though I know it

will eventually be pushed behind my ears and then finally stuffed

back into a pony-tail. I choose a simple black necklace with black,

blue, and gray beads to finish off the look. Coleman selects a solid

white, short sleeved button down shirt (with the first two buttons

open to show off some of his beautiful chest), black plain front

slacks, and his black slip-on sandals.

The doorbell rings. Kate and Moiré have returned with all

the kids, all thankfully still in one piece. Both teens stay stay for

the rest of the evening, to help the kids change their clothes for

Jolie's party and to help with entertaining them. A few minutes

before 5:00, the guests start to arrive. The first are Tricie and

Maya. Tricie walks in smiling and giving big hugs all around, and

Maya follows her in and hands me Jolie's gift. "Where is Jolie?"

Tricie asks. "We're waiting for her now; she should be here any

minute," I say as I glance over her shoulder at the front door.

Coleman makes his way to the foyer to embrace Tricie "Beatrice,

how's it going love?" "Good Cole, good." Coleman reaches down, picks up Maya and chats with her as he takes her downstairs to join the other children.

The next guests to arrive are Daneka and her fiancé Melvin. Daneka has converted back to her western clothing, which tonight is a red mock turtleneck and black denim jeans. Melvin is close to Daneka's height, with a very muscular build and disproportionately broad shoulders. He has a dark complexion and dark brown eyes, and, like his date, is wearing black denim jeans, topped with a black fitted T-shirt. We have learned that Melvin owns one of the Qwik-Stop-N-Shop stores down in the city, and that he volunteers on weekends at the local Boys and Girls Club. Watching them together, it's apparent that they have gelled and are finding their rhythm as a couple. I can tell that he and Daneka have more than values in common.

Danny makes her way to me and grabs me around the neck, hugging me tightly as she says, "I want you to meet Melvin." She takes my hand and offers it to Melvin. Melvin smiles, grabs my hand and shakes it vigorously. Daneka goes to Coleman and hugs him just as she did me. "Hey Cole, how have you been taking care

209

of my girl here?" "Been doin' my best darlin', just doin' my best."
Daneka looks at him and tilts her head to the side. "You keeping
good communication with Janice?" "That's a work in progress. We
asked her to come today, but she said she's going to Tokyo for the
week or something." Daneka then grabs Melvin by the arm and
introduces him to Coleman: "Melvin, this is Coleman, Coleman,
this is Melvin." They shake hands, exchange a bit of small talk
then head over to the bar to fix themselves a drink.

The guests steadily continue to arrive. Coleman's parents
come in, kiss Coleman, ask for their granddaughter, and then plant
themselves on the couch. I expect they'll be there for most of the
night. 5:30 comes and Coleman is beginning to get concerned
about Jolie. Her flight was a little late, but it was due to arrive at
2:30, which should still have allowed plenty of time to get here by
5:00.

The adults are enjoying the food, drinks and camaraderie,
so I go downstairs to make sure that the children are playing
constructively. While I'm downstairs, I hear the doorbell ring.

Upstairs, Coleman breaks away from the conversation he is having with a work colleague to answer the door. When he pulls it open, Janice and Jolie are standing in front of him. Jolie is excited to see her father and jumps into his arms. Coleman tucks his head close to hers and squeezes her tight while spinning her around in a circle.

Janice stands there briefly, admiring them together, and then walks into the foyer and looks around. "Nice digs – renting?" Coleman ignores her remark. "C'mon in Janice." As always, she looks impeccable and professional in a red double-breasted pantsuit over a white silk camisole, with a pale yellow scarf around her neck. Her hair is now long, almost to the middle of her back, with a barrette pulling it back away from her face.

"I thought you were going to Tokyo," Coleman says, putting Jolie down and taking her hand. "I am; I just decided to change my plans a little. I can afford to do that," Janny says pointedly. Tricie and Daneka spot Janny and make their way over for a group embrace. Janny breaks away to hug Daneka and ask, "When did you get back to the States?" She smiles radiantly at

Daneka and rubs her braids. "Yesterday." As Daneka, Janny and Tricie continue their small talk, Coleman stands to the side with Jolie and watches them enjoy each other's company. He thinks, 'It's nice to see Janice smile a genuine smile. She lights up a room when she does it.'

When I return upstairs, Jolie leaves her father and jumps into my arms. "Taylor, Taylor!" "Hi baby! My goodness, when did you get here?" "Me and my Mommy just got here." I glanced across the entry to Janny and the girls, then noticed Coleman looking admiringly at Janny. I feel immediate angst, and my heart is pounding through my shirt. I muster enough strength to walk over to Coleman, who immediately breaks his stare to look at me. The girls also break their conversation.

"I'm glad you could make it Janny," I say. Janny doesn't look at me; instead, she tells Jolie, "Get down sweetheart, you don't want to ruin your dress." Jolie goes downstairs to join the other kids. We women are all still deeply uncomfortable at this stage, so things are beyond awkward. I'm also still very self-aware during these interactions. I try to make conversation with Janice;

"Are you staying the weekend?" Janice clenches her hands together in front of her, "No, I have to leave tonight." I know my friend's body language very well and am feeling just as uncomfortable as she is. "Oh…, what time is your flight?" "I'm on the Concord, honey. It doesn't leave until I get there." Tricie interrupts, hoping to divert the conversation: "Janny, you didn't tell me you were in South Africa with Daneka."

As they begin to talk about Janny's visit, I stand aside quietly. I can feel my mind traveling away from the group. I can hear their voices and see faces, but it feels as though I'm in a tunnel and no longer in my body. I give up and slowly turn to look at Coleman, but he's gone. Somehow during my daydream, I have missed the fact that he had left the entryway. This is proving to be more difficult than I expected.

The party progresses. Jolie cuts her cake, giving me a great big hug and kiss after she does. She opens her presents, whispering in my ear, "Tell my Daddy I liked the Winnie the Pooh shirt the best!" These gestures from Jolie touch my heart. Everyone likes to be a "favorite" sometimes.

213

The children run around the house while people eat, drink, and deepen their conversations. I try to open up a dialogue with Janny a few different times, but I am cut short each and every time. Eventually, I end up in the basement with the kids, sitting Indian-style on the floor with a glass of water. Daneka catches up with me there.

"What are you drinking, girl?" Daneka asks jokingly. "Not what I'd prefer. I'm the key master tonight, so Cole gets to drink up and sleep late." Daneka sits on the floor beside me, wrapping her arm around my shoulder. "I'll tell you what Taylor, when I was gone, I missed your strength. I missed knowing that no matter what shit I went through, or how bad I felt, my Taylor was just a few miles away." I get misty and hug Daneka back. "Aw, are you trying to make me cry?" "No, I'm not, but I do want you to know that it was super duper huge of you to try and make conversation with Janny tonight. Hell, it was major that you even invited her! Those are giant steps in the right direction."

The tears I had been holding back begin to flow. "I miss our friendship, especially knowing that it will never again be what it was." "You need to let go of that pipe dream, cause you're right about that. But I think you guys have a chance. I'm not talking about a chance at a great friendship, mind you. I mean a chance that she may agree to let you both live on the planet together!" We laugh, and then we talk, reminisce, cry and watch the kids play together.

Upstairs, Coleman chats with his friends, his parents, and other guests. He eventually makes his way to the bar and grabs a beer, and then goes into the library to be alone. He doesn't know how to feel about Janice being in our home. He doesn't know how to be tactful and polite to his ex-wife, the woman he left for me.

Standing beside his desk, he notices a picture sticking out between two books on a nearby shelf. He pulls the picture out, takes a sip from his beer and looks closely at it. It's a picture of himself and Joseph on a fishing trip they took a few years ago. Trying to drown out the guilt he feels about betraying his best friend, Coleman begins to chug down the beer. He stares at the picture, lost in his own recriminations.

"If I could only read your mind right now." Coleman jerks

around, startled by Janice, who had quietly entered the room.

"Janice, how long have you been standing there?" "Not long."

Janice walks over to Coleman and takes the picture from his hand.

She looks at it then puts it down on the desk. "It hurts doesn't it?"

Coleman tries to change the subject, "Listen Janice, I don't think

we...." "What? You don't think I should be here with you?"

Coleman leans against the desk and braces himself with both

hands. She continues, "I don't think you mean that. You see, I

know you Cole. I know exactly what you want. I know you as well

as you know yourself." She walks up to Coleman and stands

between his legs. Coleman turns away. He's been drinking and

knows instinctively that this is a situation he doesn't want to be in.

Janice turns Coleman's face to hers. "Why can't I want back

what's mine?" Coleman looks into Janice's eyes, then looks away

again, and Janice turns his head to face her again. "Why are you

continuing this Cole? I lo...."

Coleman begins to walk away. Janice doesn't turn to watch

him leave. Coleman stops at the doorway, stands there for a

moment, then backs up to close the door. He sets his beer down on an end table and walks up to Janice, whose back is still turned. He holds her arms tightly at her sides and turns her around. Janice looks into his eyes and begins to cry. Coleman leans down, kisses her lightly and then pulls away. He kisses her again. Janice wraps her arms around his neck. Coleman stops and backs away, shoving his hands into his pockets. He looks at her and says, "I'm sorry Janice, but I love Taylor. I always have." "Is that right? You loved her so much that you were just kissing me, Coleman! Why don't you just stop this bullshit and come home! I've put up with your little rendezvous for 2½ years now." Coleman looks at Janice, disappointed that she is acting like she always does. "Janice, I've been drinking, you've been drinking, and this is over – right here, right now." Coleman walks out of the library and closes the door behind him.

Janice stands there for another moment to collect herself, and then leaves the library. As she walks down the hall she bumps into Daneka, who is just coming up from the basement. Daneka looks down the hall at Coleman and back at Janice, and raises her left eyebrow in suspicion. "I'm going now. I think I've had enough

fun for one night," Janny says. Tricie, who is in the dining room

making conversation with some of Coleman's friends, notices that

Janny is getting ready to leave. She approaches the two of them.

"Are you leaving?" Beatrice asks. "Yeah Bea. I'll call you guys

when I land in Tokyo."

As I reach the top of the basement stairs, I see Daneka,

Tricie and Janny all standing together. Already completely

emotionally drained, I cautiously approach the group. "I take it

you're leaving?" Janny shoots her eyes to Coleman then remarks,

"Yeah, and not soon enough, huh?" She folds her arms in front of

her chest and turns to me with a sarcastic smile. Enough is enough.

I shake my head and turn to walk away, offering my final verbal

gesture, "Have a safe flight, Janice." She reciprocates by walking

out the front door.

"This is like a really bad movie," Tricie says, amazed.

"Girl, if you only knew the half!" Daneka adds.

I want to clean house, and I mean it in more ways than one.

I begin to make my rounds, engaging small talk with guests while looking for Coleman at the same time. I soon find him outside, leaning on the deck off our bedroom. He hears the back door open but doesn't move. I walk over to him and lean on the rail beside him. "So, it wasn't too bad huh?" Coleman doesn't answer, just sips from his beer, so I continue, "Well, Janny hit me with a few pot shots. All due, I guess. I don't expect her to come in here and do and say everything I want her to. Are you okay?"

Coleman looks into the distance away from me. This is so stressful for me, and I can't begin to imagine what it's like for him, or what is on his mind. The list is far too long. Talk about a cluster fuck... I had hoped that this party might have been a way to reset the circle somehow, but clearly it didn't work. Maybe it never will. Maybe this is to be my life moving forward. I accept his silence.

"Did she change her mind about New Years?" "No baby. Listen, I got a lotta shit on my mind," Coleman waves his hand up towards the house. He knows it isn't my fault; we are all trying to keep some level of peace. He kisses me on the forehead and wraps his arm around my shoulder. We enjoy a bit more silence together.

Guests begin to leave. Another get-together under my belt.

I think things went as well as they could, and I'm actually glad that

Janny came. In my fantasy-filled mind, I had hoped that we'd at

least open up a dialogue again, even if it had to be precipitated by a

screaming match. But not this time. I'm not lucky enough for that

yet.

A week later, Coleman is on a jobsite in downtown

Richmond. He is supervising a project and spending many long

nights at the site. Unbeknownst to me, Daneka decides to visit him.

As she approaches the chain link fence, she asks a foreman where

Coleman Colebury is. The foreman gives her a hard hat and points

her in the right direction. She finds Coleman leaning on a desk,

going over blueprints with one of the architects. Surprised to see

Daneka, he smiles a big smile and gives her a hug. Daneka asks

him to go for a short walk with her to get some coffee, and he

agrees. They walk two blocks down to the Black Bean Coffee

Shop, find a table on the patio and order two coffees.

The conversation starts with nervous small talk about work,

Melvin and the kids as they sip their coffee. Daneka finally gets to the real reason she came to see him. "So how have you and Taylor been doing?" "Our relationship is beautiful. I love her to death Dan, you know that." "I don't doubt that; I just wanted to know how you guys are dealing with the stress. I mean, at the party, it was pretty thick." Coleman rests back in his seat, puts his cup down and shakes his head, looking away. "The stress is a bitch. I guess we knew that coming into it." They continue to sip from their cups. Daneka digs a little deeper: "Whose idea was it to invite Janny? It was a good one and all, but I'm just curious to know who set it in motion?" "We both thought about it, but I'm not really sure who came up with the original idea. Why? Are we playing 21 questions?" "No, I'm sorry Cole, I'm beating around the bush and I don't know why. Clearly I'm not good at it." "Well spit it out, what's on your mind, girl?" "I saw you guys coming out of the library, one behind the other, I'm guessing y'all weren't reading?" "No we weren't reading and we weren't doing nothin' else either!" Daneka crosses her arms, and waits for an explanation. "We were talking, about Jolie's visitations during the holidays." Coleman continues, hoping that Daneka will accept his explanation and not

221

continue to pry. "You realize that I do have another child, don't

you? And Janice and I will always have at least that in common."

"You're right," Daneka avers, "and I appreciate your attempt to put

me in my place." She continues with determination, "You and Tay

have such an uphill battle, I'm just here to help keep the path clear,

you know? My friends mean the world to me." "I know Daneka, I

know." Coleman is annoyed and his body language shows it.

Daneka decides to change the subject: "Melvin and I are going to

Lone Star tomorrow night, for happy hour then dinner. Why don't

you and Taylor come? Tricie's coming over after work too."

"Sounds good. About what time do you all want to get together?"

Coleman asks. "Dinner's going to have to be around 8:00 'cause

Melvin works so late, but the rest of us will be there for happy

hour first, so any time then will work." "That's good: it'll give us

enough time too." Wanting to move on from the now-tense

situation, Daneka stands up and takes her last sip of coffee.

Coleman stands to hug her goodbye. "All right baby, we'll see you

tomorrow night. I'll tell Taylor when I get home tonight." "Cool.

Later Cole." Daneka walks down the street towards her car.

Coleman sits at the table and finishes his coffee as he waits for her to leave. He desperately wants to forget the kiss he gave Janny and is working to convince himself that it didn't happen because he still has feelings for her. But what's bothering him more than anything else is, why did he let himself lose control? One of the things he enjoyed most about being away from Janice was that he had regained control over the decisions he made. Yet somehow he had allowed that power to fall into her hands again. Even worse, he is miserable about the idea of confessing that it happened, and wonders if it would be better left unsaid.

The following night, we are getting ready for the dinner date with our friends. I decide on a casual long black skirt and blue shirt. Coleman chooses black jeans and a black long-sleeved T-shirt. I'm looking forward to talking to Melvin in a more intimate setting. I spoke with him a little at Jolie's party, but since I spent the entire evening circulating and chatting with everyone there, I really don't remember the substance of our conversation.

When we arrive at the restaurant, I spot Tricie standing near the entrance. We park, then walk to the entrance to meet her.

The two of us hug. "Hey girl, how long have you been here?" I ask, hoping she had not been waiting too long. "I just got here, maybe five minutes ago." Tricie and Coleman exchange greetings. He has always felt like a big brother to her, which is how we all feel in a way, since Tricie is the "baby" of the group.

We stand in front of the restaurant making small talk while we wait for Daneka. True to form, she is running late. None of us knows Melvin well enough yet to determine whether he has that same tendency, but if he does, this could be a long wait! Happily, it's only about ten minutes later that the two of them drive up and park his huge Ford F150 truck. Melvin jumps out and walks around to let Daneka out. He grabs Daneka's hand and the two walk towards the group. Coleman is the first to reach out to Melvin and shake his hand, then me, and finally Tricie.

Inside the restaurant, we request a round table in the center of the room so we can all sit together. The meal is good, and the conversation is light. We gently "grill" Melvin, but in a manner that gives him no clue that this is what we are doing. We all share several entrees and side dishes, and consume four bottles of wine along with the food. By this time the group is very playful, so once we finish the last bottle of wine, we move on to after-dinner drinks.

At this point in the evening, a now-uninhibited Melvin is showing himself to have mighty strong opinions. It's clear that he's not afraid to share his critical views on any topic. He loses my vote when he shares his support for late-term abortions, but as he continues, things heat up even more. He begins to discuss why he believes that legalizing drugs is the answer to most of the problems inner city youths are facing. This is perfect conversation for a group of sauced liberals!

"C'mon man, you mean to tell me that you think legalizing drugs is the answer?" Coleman asks as he tears off a piece of bread and dips it into some leftover gravy. "Man, let me tell you what I see on a daily basis," says Melvin. "I see smart young brothers who don't get hired uptown, don't have the money to pay for an ivy league education, and don't get to share in the opportunities their white male counterparts have to *try* to make it. So what do they do? They start their own type of business." Melvin finishes by taking a sip of his vodka and tonic.

"That's a crock," I announce, "And while your sad, sad, story sounds sympathetic, I find it hard to believe, that you, a person who spends so much time in the community, would agree to introduce, *legally,* the same poison that's destroying that community!" Melvin takes another sip of his drink and says smugly, "Well Ms. Taylor, I'm wondering when was the last time you spent any time in that community? 'Cause it doesn't resemble anything in your neighborhood." Was this newbie taking a jab at me? I should be pissed, but I feel bruised and insulted instead. I sit back in my chair and don't respond.

Coleman makes eye contact with me. He knows I'm an emotional drunk, he also knows what's filling my plate these days, so he mouths the words "it's okay" and winks. Tricie bails out the heated conversation with, "That's not fair now, Melvin. Taylor and I both volunteer at the Mission for Hope Center every Saturday."

"Yeah, that's great – a bowl of soup sends 'em on their way to success. That's a real nice ego boost for the volunteer, but how does it help those people do for themselves?" Coleman jumps in: "Listen, listen, as long as we all continue to give back to our fellow brothers and sisters somehow, we can work it out. It's a matter of *what* you do, not whether your deeds puff your chest out more than someone else's." Melvin then argues, "Naw man, it should be what *will* you do!" He smiles, but none of us are charmed.

All this debating is working against my buzz, so I stand up and begin to gather my things. In unplanned harmony, Tricie does the same. I speak first, not really caring how sincere I sound. "I better go, we have that, um, I just need to get going." Beatrice chimes in, "Yea, I've got an early bird class tomorrow morning, so I need to get going too." Coleman looks surprised at how abrupt I am being, but he stands and pulls the chair out further for me so that I can walk away from the table. Daneka looks at us, unsettled. She recognizes the stink of BS among her friends and says, "I thought you guys were going to hang out with us." "You know how early I have to get up girl. Don't take it personally." I walk around to Danny and give her a hug. Tricie follows and reminds us, "Don't forget about the Walk for Life on Saturday." "You know I won't. Maybe I can get Melvin to come with me." Daneka wraps her arm around his shoulder. I smile. I want to say something like "that'd be great!" but I can't. For now, my tight-lipped smile will have to do the trick.

After we leave, Melvin turns to Daneka, kisses her on the mouth and asks, "You've been friends with them for how long?" Daneka smiles and answers, "A long time, why?" Melvin sits back in his chair and explains, "It's just perplexing to me that you would have friends that are so narrow-minded." Daneka crosses her arms and asks, "Excuse me?" "Don't get me wrong, they were nice and all. They're just not much like you. I would never have guessed that they'd be the type of company you'd keep, that's all." "Well damn, I'd say that's enough." Daneka is angered by his comments. She grabs her jacket "I'm ready to go, Mel." "Don't pout..." "Don't pout? You've just insulted my friends, and me for having them as my friends, and then you have the nerve to tell me not to pout?" "Yes, that's exactly what I'm doing, Daneka Smith."

Daneka turns to face Melvin squarely. "I want to tell you something, Melvin. My friends are very diverse. Our group is much like the world I live in. I surround myself with people who are *not* mirror images of myself because it keeps my life colorful and well-rounded, and if you somehow find that to be substandard, you have permission to step, now. I will not stand for you debasing me or my friends ever again." Melvin smiles, pulls his money clip from his pocket and drops cash on the table. He stands up and leads Daneka toward the door. "Did you hear me, Melvin? 'Cause I meant every word!" Melvin looks at Daneka and smiles again. "I listened to you, and I heard you."

On the way home, Coleman and I have a conversation about Melvin. "He's pretty extreme. I mean, no care for human life, and what's all that crap about selling drugs and businessmen?" Coleman adds, "Yea, I've always thought your girl Daneka is intense, but he's really out there." "I let him get to me though, and I don't want to do that again," I say. "If this is the man Daneka loves, I need to accept him wholeheartedly." Coleman jokes, "Yeah right, Ms. That's-a-crock!" Coleman smiles a big smile and kisses me on the cheek. "Well, he astounded me when he suggested that I don't understand or give back to the community. He just met me! I think he was looking at the packaging, ya know? Not what's going on inside of me. We just met tonight, so he still needs time to figure out if he hates me or not!" I smile. "It's impossible to hate you – you're like candy!" "Tell that to Janny." Coleman glances up and the mood turns somber.

Maybe that buzz is still working... I continue, "I would give anything to be able to have a relationship with her again." "Why do you feel that way? You still have Beatrice and Daneka." I am taken-aback by Coleman's suggestion. "Coleman, you may not miss her as an ex-wife, but that has nothing to do with me missing her as a friend. Don't you miss Joseph?" "Yea, but men are different. I can't do anything about that." "Have you tried, Cole?" "Look Taylor, I said men are different. I stole my man's wife from him, so not only does he not want me as a friend; he doesn't want to see my face again, ever. Hell, my demise couldn't come soon enough for Joe. Probably yours, too." I absorb the harsh truth of Coleman's remarks, and I agree with part of what he is saying. But it still doesn't have much to do with my desire for a relationship of some type with Janny. I love her.

I've been sensing recently that Coleman is going through a lot inside. We've overcome a lot and grown closer as a couple, but our reality is still a bitch and our life is still hard. And I've sensed

more stress in my husband since Jolie's party. When he's at home,

he spends a lot of time in his office, listening to music and just

sitting quietly. He isn't ignoring me or the kids, and has remained

attentive, but he's mentally struggling with something. I've asked

him on a couple of different occasions if Janny is still planning on

moving back to Virginia. His answer is always the same: "She

hasn't said anything else." I've decided that if Coleman wants to

talk to me about it, he'll come to me, so I'm done asking.

It's now the morning of Dawn's fall concert. And somehow

in the midst of all the madness, the main thing on my mind is

whether or not Joseph is going to show up. He hasn't called to

respond, and as always I want Dawn's experience to be good.

Dawn is certainly hoping he will be there. Jolie also arrived this

morning and can't wait to see her Uncle Joseph.

The enormous elephant in the room, of course, is the funk

between Joseph and Coleman. They haven't been face-to-face

since Janny's infamous party. So this night could go off without a

hitch, or it could fail miserably. Or, we could achieve something in the gray area between these two outcomes, which was a more realistic goal. I was longing for that gray area.

We arrive with the kids in tow a half-hour early. Dawn must go warm up with her classmates. In front of the school, Dawn jumps into my arms and wraps her arms tightly around my neck, then jumps down and runs in with a group of girls. Coleman turns to ask me, "Do you want me to take these guys in?" "Yes, I'll wait here for Joe." He hands the baby to me and takes Jolie, Bailey and Joe Jr. inside. I stand just inside the foyer, looking back and forth for Joseph, but as it gets closer to 6:00 I feel less and less optimistic. Unbeknownst to me, Joseph is sitting in his car in the parking lot, trying to decide whether or not he can handle seeing Cole and me together.

Five minutes before the program is to start, I give up. As I turn to walk inside the auditorium with Daniel, I hear Joseph call out, "Taylor!" I turn around to see Joseph walking quickly towards me. I smile as he approaches, and we hug. "I'm so glad you came!" Joseph smiles halfheartedly then explains, "Listen, I can't stay." My smile fades as I tilt my head, flustered. "Why?" Joe then admits, "I thought I could do this Tay, but I can't. I love my children, more than you can imagine, but it's too fuckin' humiliating. I sat in my car tonight and watched you guys, I watched him with *my* children, mine! And it made my blood boil." I turn away. "I'm moving out west, Taylor." "What do you mean, out west? So, you're just gonna pack up with my kids and leave cuz you can't deal?" "I can't, I won't, and I'm doing this for me. We'll make it work with the kids." Reacting to my anger, Daniel starts to cry. "Oh, and what a great time to bring all of this up Joe. This is just awesome! Let me just go in here and enjoy the show huh?" I turn my back and walk into the theatre, shushing the baby. Joseph turns simultaneously and we walk away from each another.

I slowly make my way to my seat and settle in with Daniel on my lap. I turn toward Coleman and whisper the critical details of my conversation with Joseph. I want empathy and I want to scream. Mostly, though, I want to hate Joseph for trying to live his life outside of my overwhelming shadow. I want to be selfish and have him keep me comfortable even in his deep pain, but I can't. I still love him, and the way he loves our children. A few minutes later, I glance behind me and notice that Joseph is standing at the back of the auditorium, quietly watching. His eyes meet mine, and I feel a rush of emotion. I am so deeply sorry. I place my finger over my mouth and say the words "I'm sorry" and point to him. He looks down, and doesn't respond. I don't expect him to. I know that his intention is to watch Dawn's performance and leave.

Coleman searches my tear-stained face. He looks back and sees Joseph. He gets up and leaves our row to approach him, climbing the three flights of steps between them. As he grows nearer, Coleman notices Joseph's uptight stance. "Wassup, man?" Joseph looks Coleman up and down and doesn't answer. Coleman continues, "I want to talk to you for a sec, man." "Look Coleman, I ain't here to talk to you, I'm here to see my daughter, then I'm out." Coleman looks at the stage, then turns back to Joseph. "Listen Joe, Dawn's not on until near the end of show. This will only take a second." Coleman opens the door. Joseph walks out, shoving his hands into his pockets.

Coleman begins to speak first; "Look, I know you don't want to hear what I have to say, but taking the kids away from

Taylor isn't going to make things any easier." "Man, you must be trippin' if you think I'm gonna listen to you." Coleman reaches out to stop Joseph by grabbing his arm. Joseph turns around and swings at Coleman, hitting him in the face. The two begin to fight, scuffling through the front doors and into the parking lot. They go after each other until the school security guard breaks them up. "Look, you two can take this back to wherever you came from. You will *not* be allowed to continue this behavior here. There's a show going on. I'll let you go this time, but if anything else happens I'll become Robocop and trust me, you don't want that."

Joseph and Coleman stand, straighten their clothes and dab at the various cuts and scrapes on their hands and faces. Joseph turns to Coleman. "This shit is fucked up, man. We were *boys*, and *boys* don't do shit like this to each other! I can't believe you." Joseph points to the theatre. Coleman says sadly, "I'm sorry, man, I am sorry. I know you don't forgive me for being with Taylor but what I'm asking, I'm not asking for me. I'm asking for her, man. Don't you see? This isn't about me – it's about your kids."

Joseph tries not to listen but he does hear. "The way me and Taylor came to be was a big-ass mess. Shit, I know that. But I love her, man, and she has spent the last two years in therapy trying to make things right with herself. I'm afraid that if you take her kids away, that far away, she may not make it through that. She's the mother of your kids, man, the mother of your kids."

"She acted like a fucking whore! And you were right there by her side, enjoying the returns." Coleman's shoulders slump as he accepts that this conversation isn't going anywhere. He continues, "Your opinion is yours, you can think and say what you want, you can try to cut her ass up with your words and your actions, Joe. But if you take her kids that far away, then you're just being spiteful and you know it." Coleman walks back to the auditorium. Joe follows a few steps behind, getting inside the door just in time to catch Dawn's performance. When she finishes, he goes backstage to congratulate her and give her flowers. He is serious about this move, but he doesn't want to devastate his children or their mother. He decides that he'll discuss it with the children before he comes to a final decision.

13 COMING TO TERMS

Janice's birthday party visit and Joseph's impending move to California have contributed to a heightened tension between Coleman and me. We have become terse in our conversations, and we spend less and less of our leisure time together. Coleman works in his study for hours on end, while I busy myself with work at home and at the center. I hate the way things are going. We've gone through so much devastation together, and at one time that brought us closer. Now I feel a strained distance, and this is something I have never felt with him before, not even when we were just friends.

It's the morning of the Crisis Connection Walk for Life, and this is Joseph's week with the kids, so I open my eyes at about

5:30 to find a quiet house and Coleman sitting in the chair at our bedroom window. I get up and walk over to Coleman to ask, "What are you thinking about, love?" Coleman puts his book down on the ledge, pauses for a moment, and then answers "I was just thinking to myself how lucky I am to have my wife and my family, and although we can't be whole all of the time, I'm willing to make that sacrifice for the wrongs I committed during my marriage to Janice. I just never expected the emotional side to be so difficult."

I am suddenly uneasy about what he might say next. "What are you saying, Cole? Are you... are you still in love with Janice?" Coleman looks up at me and doesn't answer. He then drops his head and says, "I'm not sure what I feel for her. I'm so sorry Taylor, I wish I had a better answer, but I don't." I instantly feel sick to my stomach. I study his face and wait for what seems like an eternity for him to recant, or for me to wake up from this nightmare, but neither happens. After this deafening hush, I hear myself say sternly, "Then you should leave." I brace myself against the windowsill and stand before him, and again I wait. My heart aches for him to say, "no," or that he is confused or afraid, but each silent moment passes with nothing from Coleman.

I stomp across the room, grabbing yesterday's wrinkled T-shirt from a chair. I grab my gym shorts from the day before off the floor and pull them on. I slide my feet into flip flops and walk into the bathroom, searching frantically through the drawers for a hair elastic. Where the fuck are they? All I need is a goddamn hair tie! I find one and pull my hair back into a ponytail as I glance up at the mirror. I see a fool, a stupid fool who actually believed this could work. A fool who hoped that that maybe, just maybe, her happy ending just required two left turns to get to instead of a straight line. I can't stand to look at myself. I throw my brush onto the counter and scream, "YOU COWARD!" I sob aloud, so angry for losing this fight, for losing my love. I must now face the fear that I have been wrong about Coleman and my choices. I run down the stairs and jump into the Suburban, back out of the driveway and roar away. Where I am going, I have no idea. I'm in shock from what has just taken place. In spite of all I have sacrificed and all I've been through, I am still going to end up without the man I love.

I walk up to Tricie and Daneka, who are standing together waiting amidst the growing crowd of participants at the corner of Jessup and Colver Streets. My swollen eyes are covered with sunglasses, but my disheveled appearance and dispirited demeanor is not easy to hide. "Hey, guys." I try to rush in for a quick hug before either of them can take a good look at me. It doesn't work. "Damn girl, you look like hell!" Daneka removes my sunglasses and looks at my face. "Thanks, you look good too. Where's Melvin?" I take my sunglasses back and hurry to put them back on my face. "He's working today. Where's Coleman?" "He's uh... got some things to do, and he has Daniel, so..."

Tricie interrupts, "Well guys, I gotta get this walk started so I'll meet you at the starting line." Tricie steps up to the podium to give a brief welcome, explain how the proceeds will be used, and state the rules of the walk. She then blows the starting whistle and the walkathon begins. I clap as my friend finishes her speech. I am so proud of all that she's accomplished. She has grown so much in the face of so much pain. She is finding new purpose in her life, new things to give her life meaning. Tricie walks over to join Daneka and me. I wave my hand saying "Let's go ladies!"

As we wrap our arms around each others' shoulders to begin, Daneka looks to her right and sees Janny approaching. I didn't know she was going to join us, but I have a feeling that Janny knew I was going to be here. Although it feels like they allowed Janny more time to prepare for this meeting, I'm sure our friends are probably just trying to help us connect again. Tricie breaks the silence with, "What took you so long? I told you to be here at a quarter 'til." "A friend of mine called. He needs a place to stay." I snap my head around in Janny's direction, knowing damn well who this "friend" is. I play along: "And what did you say?" Janny smiles in a sexy way, winks and says, "Darlin', you know I never turn my friends away." She turns her back and begins to walk. Tricie jogs to catch up to her.

I stand there, paralyzed and defeated, and begin to cry. Daneka wraps her arm around me and says, "What is going *on*, Tay?" "It's just overwhelming right now Daneka. It's too much. I can't take this." "We didn't tell you Janny was coming 'cause we knew you wouldn't come if you knew. If it makes you that uncomfortable, we can leave. I'll go with you." "I'm okay, I'll be alright." And I will be all right. I'm going to will myself to be all right. To hell with this! It isn't the worst I have ever been through.

We finish the walk. Tricie stays at the park for the festivities and cleanup, Daneka meets up with Melvin for lunch, Janny stays back with Tricie, and I go home. So far, this day has been mentally exhausting. I am hoping that Coleman will be at home, ready to tell me that he knows unequivocally what he wants, and that it's me. Another part of me wants him to stay gone so that if the decision is that he wants to be with her, he'll be doing it for the right reasons, his reasons.

I open the door to a still home. It's frighteningly quiet. I drop my keys on the bench by the door and walk upstairs, dragging my feet down the hall to my room like a dead man walking. As I enter our bedroom, my eyes are fixed on the bed, which is unchanged and exactly how I left it. My breaths are as quick as my heartbeats as I realize that Coleman's side of the closet is empty. I take in this evidence of his absence as dysphoria and rage race through my body and mind simultaneously. I notice something on my pillow, a note. I walk over and pick it up with my now trembling hands. It reads:

Taylor,

You have my heart, and I do love you, more than I ever thought I could love someone. This I know. But I'm having a hard time separating myself from Janny and Jolie. I don't know what to make of them being together and apart from me. I wish I could have done everything perfectly for you, and I wish I could feel exactly how you want me to. But I don't, and I can't lie to you anymore.

PS: Daniel is with your mother."

I crumple the note and sweep my open hand violently toward the nearby bedside table to send the lamp and a vase of flowers flying through the air and crashing to the floor. All the aggression flowing through my body goes into this swing, and I'm breathing heavily as if I've been running for miles. I stand there, staring down at the broken, wet, dripping mess on the floor that's a perfect metaphor for my life now.

After a while I pick up the phone to call Janny's condo. I feel the need to confirm that she was referring to Coleman at the Crisis Connection walk. I dial the number, wait a few short moments and decide to hang up. Do I really want to know? I'm about to turn off the phone when I hear the click of someone answering. I hear, "Janice speaking." I stand quietly and wait, my mind tortured about what I should do next. Janny clearly suspects that it is me, because she says loudly, "Coleman, I think this might be for you." There is silence, then I hear Coleman's voice, "Hello?" I drop the phone as if it's on fire, Coleman's voice repeats through the phone, over and over.

At Janny's condo, Coleman asks, "Who was that?" Janny, sitting at her makeup table, continues brushing her hair as she says, "I don't know... did you tell anyone you were going to be here?" Feeling miserable, Coleman shakes his head. "No, no I didn't." Janny enjoys the fact that he's refusing to mention his wife. She smiles crookedly at her reflection, puts down her brush and walks to the door. She grabs her suitcase with her back to him. "Well, I'm going. Stay as long as you like, just make sure to have Hildie come and clean on Monday, Wednesday and Friday, and remind her to water the plants." She turns back to face him. "And don't put your feet on the coffee table, dear. That marble is imported from Italy. It may have been a while, and I know you've undergone a change in taste, but I have not." Janny walks out, slamming the door behind her. Staring blankly at the door, Coleman plops down on the sofa, uses the remote to turn on the television, and rests his feet directly on the coffee table.

I spend the following day contemplating whether or not to call Coleman. His truth is difficult to accept, and at the heart of my emotions is a great distress. Will I be able to pick myself up and put the pieces of my life back together again?

Meanwhile, outside my door, life continues on. Daneka wants to have a dinner on Wednesday night, just a simple get-together so that her family and Melvin's can meet. I have taken the event on as a welcome distraction and have agreed to host it at my house. But in the meantime, the lonely minutes feel like days.

The following evening, I'm sitting home alone eating a dinner that I have no appetite for. The phone rings, and I cautiously pick it up. At first, there is silence, then a small voice says, "Hi Mommy!" It's Bailey, calling from Joseph's house. I'm relieved to hear her voice. "Hi sweetheart! I'm here, I'm here baby." I exhale through a giggle, calming my emotions with the sweet sound of her voice. "I miss you Mommy." "And I miss you, love bug." I wipe my tear-stained face. Bailey begins to share her news: "Daddy wants to move to California, and he said he's gonna talk to you about letting me go too." My stomach churns with uneasiness. I am being bombarded with tests: tests of my coping ability, tests of my tenacity, tests of my love. "What do you think?" I ask her. Bailey says, "Well, I thought about it a lot, and I think I want to go." I am sickened by the thought of my oldest child living so far away. What are you doing to me, God? Is this my punishment? Because I'm surely not going to survive much more of this. My life has been a marathon of despair since Cole left. There are no longer levels of high or low; instead it's one big messy pile of turmoil and misery. "Mom, are you there?" "I'm here baby. I'm proud of you for thinking through your decision. Your Dad and I will discuss it..." my voice is faint, weak. I would cry but I have no tears. "Dad said I could go to a private school. It's called Grayson Academy, it's a nice school, and I wanna go there." I am having trouble focusing, and I can barely process Bailey's conversation. I do hear her say goodnight, and as much as I love my daughter, this is a relief, because I no longer want to keep up a happy façade. We say our goodnights. I can accept the part I played in disrupting my family, but this doesn't magically make things easier. Part of me still feels like Joe is taking the kids away just to hurt me, but the rational side of me knows that he needs to make this move to flourish in his own life. The emotional friction all around me is reaching a crescendo.

The night of Daneka's gathering brings a change of pace. Coleman greets me with a dismissive kiss, but I let it be. I make small talk, not asking the questions I really want answers to, for fear of "rocking the boat." Coleman, on the other hand, keeps reiterating his love for me, and his guilt for harboring affection for his family life with Janice and Jolie. I want my husband back, but at this point he sounds like Charlie Brown's teacher, the muffled horn. I cut the conversation short and muster the strength to tell him he can have one more week to think things over. I need to set limits for my own good, so I can find my own peace.

Now that all of Daneka and Melvin's guests are here, we start the evening with cheeses and rosé. There is a pleasant ambient hum in the house, the sounds of people chatting, nibbling and enjoying themselves. Janice arrives at about 7:20 and is her usual self. She is also the only one of the three of us who seems comfortable with our situation. She makes her rounds, more calm and collected than any politician. She knows how to handle herself in a crowd, even under duress. As Janny says, "These days, you can't tell a CEO from an average Joe, so you should accord everyone the same respect." She has always had the stuff that corporate giants are made of.

As the self-proclaimed "mother" of the group, I sense a distance developing between Melvin and Daneka. It is already evident in their body language, and my gut tells me that the reason will reveal itself at some point in the evening. I watch Melvin and his family interact. He is a carbon copy of his father, right down to his style of clothing and insufferable wit. During the meal I can sense Daneka tiring of both men's stingy and ill-mannered comments. I turn my attention to Melvin's mother, who is the epitome of female submission. Her eyes are fixed on Melvin, and she is constantly adjusting, dusting, and tidying his appearance. It seems that tidying is her obsession – the next morning I realize that at some point during the evening Melvin's mother had rearranged my cutlery drawer, tidied up the downstairs bathroom and spruced up the children's playroom! I can see now where many of Melvin's attitudes come from. Unfortunately, they are quite different from Daneka's.

The table conversation has gone well so far, but I am on edge anyway. I feel like the stiffness between Danny and Melvin is going to come to a head – the air is thick with tension. As the entrees are served, the conversation takes a turn for the worse. Melvin senior speaks to me directly; "Taylor, your home is quite nice, did you build or buy?" "Thank you. My husband designed it, and then we had it built." Melvin junior adds, "So you kept it in the family *and* you kept it real." Coleman adds, "The last time I checked I was about as real as it gets." He smiles, crossing his hands in front of him. Melvin junior then continues with, "You know what I mean. Who did you use as your subcontractor? Were they black-owned or white-owned?" Coleman carefully answers, "The majority of the men were black." Melvin junior retorts, "Of course, the meat-and-potato guys usually are, but who was on top? Who was the cream on the top, Cole? All white? Or did you guys make the time in your busy schedules to sift through and look for the ones owned by brothas and sistas?" Melvin senior looks at Melvin junior and raises one eyebrow, as if to send him a high five. I put my fork down and bury my head in my hands. This guy is simply an asshole, and I'm in no mood for this.

Daneka insists that he verbally change course; "Melvin, just drop it, okay?" But Melvin senior picks up where his ol' boy son left off. "We have to remember to support our brothers at all cost." Melvin junior then adds, "Even if it means you don't put all your money into the so-called *better* neighborhoods." "Man, if I didn't know better I'd think you were jealous," says Coleman. "I live where I choose to live, not where I feel pressured to live. Don't fault me for my success." Janny looks at Coleman and interjects, "Oh, is *that* what you're calling it now?" Coleman snaps his head in Janny's direction, surprised that she's reinforcing the Graham's rhetoric. Mrs. Graham rises to her feet, "Well now, who's ready for dessert?" She had put a polite end to the discussion and shown us all who actually wears the pants in that family. Nevertheless, we all feel awkward since we haven't even touched our dinners yet.

Tricie speaks up, "With all due respect Mr. Graham and Melvin, we all do our share to support our communities. I mean, we do our best to make a difference because we want to be able to look ourselves in the mirror and be proud!" "Give me a break. When you look in the mirror you're looking at the most confused sister in the room." Daneka stands and says, "Melvin!" but he continues, "I mean c'mon, you didn't stop with just one white boy, you had to keep on 'til you got it right." Tricie covers her mouth in shock, finding it hard to believe that he could be so insulting.

Daneka yells, "That's enough! I have heard my fill. Now you, your noncommittal copycat father, and your pitiful June-Cleaver-wannabe mother can take your sorry asses out of my friend's home!" Daneka removes the engagement ring from her finger and slams it down on the table in front of Melvin. "I told you before that I would never allow you to mistreat my friends again. Why don't you take a good look at yourself? You're so quick to tell everyone else what they're doing wrong, but you don't give thought to your own faults. If you can act like this big of a jerk before we even tie the knot, I am taking it upon myself to loosen the strings before we ever do!" Janny breaks the silence with slow, steady applause. She casually takes a sip of her wine and remarks, "Taylor, I gotta give it to you, you sure as hell can throw a party." 'What a mess,' I think to myself, 'what a mess.'

Melvin and his family leave, then Coleman quietly leaves as well. I go to Daneka and wrap my arm around her shoulder. "Dan, I am so sorry. I tried to make it nice for you. I put my heart into this for you." Janny snipes, "You put your heart and many other things into places they don't belong, don't you Taylor?" I don't comment, but Tricie does. "Don't, Janny. This isn't about you." I try to stay on course: "Do you want to maybe go and talk with him?" Daneka shakes her head. "No, I can't have anyone that judgmental around me, and I'd be a fool to think that he'll change for me. I mean, look at his father!"

The girls all stay on a while. Janny wanders out to the porch and leans against the rail. She gazes at the stars as the night air envelops her. When Daneka finds the right moment, she approaches Janny and stands at her side with her elbows on the rail. She too gazes up, taking in the beautifully clear night. "It's chilly out here." "Yeah, it is," Janny agrees. "A lot like your mood tonight," Daneka admonishes. "Can't help it if I'm good at it. Now wait a minute – you're not out here to try and tell me *I'm* the bad girl here!" "No, I'm not trying to say you're anything, Janny. But I do want to ask what you are doing." Janny shakes her head in irritation. "Excuse me?" "At Jolie's party, I saw you and Coleman come out of the library. What exactly are you up to, Janice?" "He was my husband first. I can't help it if he doesn't know how to let go." Daneka then says "Really Janice? Or is it *you* who really knows how to hold on?"

Janny looks away, so Daneka continues, "I look at us sometimes and I can't believe the way we are now, compared to the way we used to be. What went down between Coleman and Taylor was some fucked-up shit, but what I'm feeling about Melvin is nothing compared to what they have to live with every day. And what you all are doing right now isn't making it any easier for Bailey, Dawn, Jolie, Joe Jr., and Daniel." Janny interrupts "Are you done?" Daneka knows that this is Janny's way of preventing Danny from seeing her with her guard down, so she continues, "Let it go, Janny. Let *him* go. You need to hear this from someone who loves you, so I'm telling you – he loves Taylor. Game over." Daneka turns away and goes back into the house. Janny turns back around, braces herself on the railing, and cries quietly.

Janny leaves the house a few minutes later and goes for a drive in the country to plan her next steps. After an hour or so, she parks at her condo, where Coleman is still staying. It is now a little after 2:00 in the morning. She walks in the door and is surprised to find Coleman sitting on the couch. It's show time. Janny pauses for a moment, then walks over to the window and pulls the curtains back as she announces, "I want you out – today." Coleman looks up at Janny. She continues, "I think you're having a hard time making your decision, so I'll make it for you. You've chosen your wife, so go." Coleman stands and tries to take her hand in his. For a brief moment, she fancies the idea of pulling him close to her and taking him into her arms, but she brushes his hand away and strides to her closet to pull out one of her furs. Her voice begins to waver, but she forges on: "You know one thing I love about Washington? The many months of cold. I get much more use out of these." Coleman breaks his silence. "Janny, I.." but Janny walks abruptly to the door and snatches it open. "Goodbye Coleman." She walks out. Coleman stands frozen in place for a moment, then finally walks over to the window to watch Janny exit the front door and get into her car. She starts the engine and drives off without hesitation.

This is the way many of Janny's decisions are; impetuous and immediate. Coleman pulls the drapes together to close them. He walks into the back bedroom and stands in the doorway, staring at his bags, the bags he had packed the night before in preparation for leaving.

I am also wide awake, working in the rose beds in my front yard. I have my back turned and hear a car drive up. I turn to see who is pulling into the driveway this early. It's Janny. She walks briskly up to me. I stand there quietly, not knowing what to expect. She speaks first. Looking beyond me at the rose bed she says, "Even now, you still do that crap yourself. You'll never learn." Her attempt at humor makes me so happy that my eyes begin to fill with tears, but I just listen.

"You know I never did take well to hostile takeovers. I guess this situation with you and Coleman is just one I have to deal with." I bite my lip, then wipe my tears. Janny shakes her head in disbelief and admits, "You were my best friend, Taylor. I knew about you two when Cole and I started dating, but I thought I could keep my marriage together. Goddammit, I never thought your stupid little heart would get in the way of my business savvy!" Not wanting to face me anymore, she looks away, now beginning to cry herself, "I miss you, but I'm not ready to deal with you yet," she says as she directs her hands between us. "Whenever you're ready, Janny." Janny turns to me and inspects my face, taking in all that I am offering her. In that silence I approach, wrap my arms around her and hold her tight, not knowing when, or if, I'll have this chance again. She raises her arms slowly to hug me and cries a little, then reverts back to her old self. She pulls away and walks back to her car, opens the door, gets in and drives away.

I go into the house, stopping at the half-bath on the main floor to wash my face. As I walk into the kitchen to get a towel for my face, I hear the screen door open. I turn and see Coleman walking in the door slowly, as if to make sure that it's okay. Unsure if I can accept this, I lean against the counter. Coleman lets the door close against his back. He looks me over, bows his head for a moment, then walks up to me. He stands in front of me and cups his hands under my elbows to lift me onto the counter. In the silence, his actions speak volumes.

I want so much right now. I want him to console me and tell me that he's done wrong. I want him to cradle me in his arms and promise never to hurt me again. I want him to wake me from this horrible nightmare so that we can relive that horrible day the right way. Instead, he gently wipes the hair from my face and simply says, "I'm so sorry, and I want to come home." And that is all.

And maybe that simplicity is enough. Maybe my grandiose ideas of the perfect life are just that: far too grand. I grab Coleman's face and hold it, to make sure that he is looking directly into my eyes. Only the answer to one question will satisfy me right now. "Is this the home where your heart is?" Coleman responds without hesitation, "This is the home where my *soul* is." We kiss.

I believed at the time that the day Coleman and I married on Jefferson Lake was the beginning of our new life. I now know that we started somewhere in the middle, and that our true beginning has come after a great deal of pain, heartache and misunderstanding. I also know that I will never have the kind of perfect ending that my dinner parties achieved in the past, and I accept that. Our marriage is a work in progress, and we are just like everyone else who lives behind a white picket fence. The stories may be different, but every couple is forced to deal with doses of reality.

Within a month's time, Joseph moves to California, buys a house and prepares for Bailey's arrival, while I help her prepare for her new life in California on my end. Joseph and I have agreed that Bailey will live with him for as long as she wants, and in the event that she doesn't like it, she will come back home to live with me. For now, Dawn and Joe Jr. will visit him as often as they like, but will stay with me full-time until they are each old enough to make permanent decisions of their own. Joseph has also revealed that his girlfriend Margaret has moved out to California as well. Bailey likes her. Apparently she displays more of a playful side, which Joseph lacks.

On the day of the move, Coleman, the children and I sit in the front yard waiting for Joseph to arrive. Bailey asks, "Mom, you're not going to cry are you?" "Yes, but I won't blubber." I smile and kiss Bailey on the forehead. Coleman sits beside me and smiles and hugs me close for support. We watch Joseph drive up to the front of the house with Margaret. They park and walk arm-in-arm to the porch. We stand to greet them properly. Margaret is statuesque, eye-to-eye with Joseph in height. She has short light brown hair cut in a pixie cut, and piercing jet-black eyes, which are in striking contrast to her hair. She is simply dressed in a baby-blue V-neck t-shirt, white shorts and flip-flops, and is a very attractive woman.

Bailey springs to her feet as her dad approaches, as do Joe Jr. and Dawn. They climb up their father's body, using his arms and legs like tree limbs. Margaret confidently walks up to me and extends her hand. I happily embrace her. "It's so nice to meet you!" "You too." I turn to introduce my husband. "This is Coleman. Cole, this is Margaret." The two shake hands. Joseph sets the children down and makes his way over to us. He greets Coleman, "'Sup man?" and keeps his attention directed on the kids. Coleman extends his hand in affection, "What's up man, flight good?" "Good, good." Then, realizing that Joseph, Margaret and I will need a minute alone, Coleman scoops Daniel up and takes him into the house. I kneel down to Bailey, wipe her face and promise, "You can come home anytime you like, okay? And call me every day, anywhere. You know all the numbers by heart, right?" I can feel my voice cracking. Bailey scolds me, "Mom!" "I'm not blubbering yet." We hug, an embrace I don't want to let go. Margaret then says, "I'll walk Bailey to the car." They walk away, leaving Joseph and me standing alone.

I try to read Joseph's face as I wipe mine. He has a healthier, more peaceful look about him. I suppose he's further along on this part of our familial journey, and I can't help but think to myself that for him this move to California is for the best. "You look good on her," I say about Margaret, lightly touching my hand to his hair. "She looks good on *me*," Joe adds. I plead gently, "Please take care of my baby..." Joseph, feeling near tears himself, kisses me on the forehead and whispers in my ear, "You take care of *yourself*." He leans down to kiss Dawn and Joe Jr. goodbye, then walks briskly to his car. Bailey is sitting in the back seat, her eyes fixed on mine and her hand pressed against the window. I raise my hand, running down the sidewalk as their car pulls away. I want Bailey's last visual memory of me to be there, solidly right there. I want Bailey to always know in her heart that what she saw fading in the distance will always be waiting for her.

When the car disappears from sight, I drop down to Dawn and Joe Jr. and hug them tight. Coleman walks out and delivers Daniel to me. I hold my children, kissing them and smearing my tears of pain on their sweet little faces. When I can break away, I look up at Coleman. "I guess that's the way it is." His expression shows his agreement. This is the way it will be. I will have to work on that fence, because it's an illusion after all, just like my marriage to Joseph had been, and like Coleman's to Janny. At that moment I realize that it's time to get rid of my fairy-tale white picket fence and embrace what's real; my beloved children who cuddle here in my lap, and the man I love who is standing right in front of me. They have given me that sense of purpose and completeness I longed for.

I've been through so many hard and painful lessons recently, and this is just one more to add to the pile. I could feel sorry for myself and worry about the struggles to come, but instead, I choose to close my eyes and silently say a prayer,

"...thank you God, for my health, my life with all its imperfections, and my children. Thank you for Joseph, who has been man enough to let me go, because for that, I'll never forget him. Thank you for teaching me how to love, and showing me how it feels to be loved; and thank you for Coleman, who is helping me achieve my version of a normal, happy life, with or without a white picket fence."

End

ABOUT THE AUTHOR

LEAH MCCLURE is a writer with a newly discovered rich ancestry. She spent the first 19 years of her life growing up in West Haven Connecticut, which is where her colorful imagination and love of writing began. In grade school she wrote her first book which caught the eye of her teacher. Play's, poems, short stories and children's books soon followed. The following 25 years she spent between Richmond and the City of Falls Church Virginia. Five of Leah's favorite gifts from God are her 4 children and her husband of 10 years. This is Leah's first book to be published, which she wrote on a word processor while her 2 oldest children were both toddlers! Leah now resides in Massachusetts with her husband where on one hand she can hone her love of the Winter season, but on the other hand she can battle against the Red Sox with her love of the Yankees.

Made in the USA
Middletown, DE
05 May 2022

65354283R00163